Honeymoon for One

Lisa R. Schoolcraft

Honeymoon for One

Lisa R. Schoolcraft

Printed in the United States of America

First Printing, 2021

ISBN-13: 978-1-7339709-3-8

Cover Design: Brittany Jordan

Publisher: Schoolcraft Ink LLC

Visit the author's website at www.schoolcraftink.com

Table of Contents

Chapter 1 1

Chapter 2 13

Chapter 3 25

Chapter 4 36

Chapter 5 47

Chapter 6 55

Chapter 7 67

Chapter 8 79

Chapter 9 89

Chapter 10 106

Chapter 11 116

Chapter 12 131

Chapter 13 140

Chapter 14 146

Chapter 15 158

Chapter 16 167

Chapter 17 174

Chapter 18 182

Chapter 19 192

Chapter 20 202

Chapter 1

Ravyn Shaw awoke early New Year's Day 2016, preparing to run Atlanta Track Club's Resolution Run. She crept around the bedroom as she put on her running clothes, using the dim light of her phone to find what she needed. She was trying not to wake her boyfriend Marc Linder.

Her boyfriend. Ravyn could hardly believe how her life had changed in the past two months. She had moved into Marc's house the month before, shortly before Christmas. She was finding it difficult being comfortable in her new home. She honestly considered it more Marc's home, not theirs.

She had yet to hang some of her favorite art on the walls. She'd barely been able to salvage her pictures, wall hangings and posters when her belongings had been destroyed by mice in a storage unit. Thankfully, the mice had been unable to reach many framed artworks, but there had been some gnaw marks on the wood.

The 4-mile race that morning was held in Atlanta's Brookhaven neighborhood, right at the Brookhaven train station. By living with Marc, Ravyn would have a shorter drive to get to the race start.

Marc stirred next to her. "You're up? What time is it?"

"Yes, I have the race this morning. Go back to sleep."

Marc rolled over and touched Ravyn's back as she sat on the bed. "Happy New Year."

"Happy New Year," she said, bending down to kiss the top of his head. "I should be back around noon, I guess."

"Want to go to lunch after?"

"Sure. Sounds good."

"Love you," Marc said.

"Love you, too."

With the race early New Year's day, Ravyn just wanted to stay home for the holiday. They barely stayed awake to midnight to share a kiss and a sip of prosecco.

Ravyn thought about her living situation for the entire 4-mile race that morning. She wasn't entirely unhappy living with Marc. She liked that she had someone to talk to when she came home at night. But she hated her longer commute from his house to her office downtown and back again.

In Atlanta, even a few miles could add hours to a commute.

She liked that Marc had said she could begin to find new paint, new decor and new curtains for the house, which hadn't been upgraded since his first marriage ended several years ago.

They'd agreed on a kind of cream paint they would apply over Martin Luther King Jr. weekend. She thought about what supplies she'd need to pick up for that project as she ran.

She was also glad she'd talked Marc out of a similar beige paint to match his dark brown leather furniture. Ravyn had wanted more contemporary colors. Truth be told she'd like to see the end of his 1990s leather furniture, too.

Ravyn was having a hard time keeping her gray tomcat Felix from scratching on the leather couch. She and Marc had already argued about Felix using his couch as a scratching post.

Ravyn did have a cat tree for Felix. And she'd tried to keep him in the guest bedroom when they both were at work.

It wasn't her fault that Felix liked Marc's leather furniture better than the cat tree. No matter how much she sprayed Feliway on the furniture, Ravyn could not get Felix away from that leather.

Ravyn remembered when she first got Felix from an animal shelter. The shelter had said he was a "young cat" but he was definitely more a kitten. At least he acted like one.

She brought him home to her condo in Midtown and he'd climbed into her dishwasher as she was emptying it. Then he cried because he couldn't figure out how to get out over the dishwasher rack.

Another time, she'd been making scrambled eggs for breakfast, going in and out of the refrigerator. Suddenly she heard him crying but couldn't figure out where he was.

Ravyn opened a nearby closet and the small pantry in her kitchen before opening the refrigerator door. There was Felix, his gray face looking up at her.

Ravyn was lost in her memories as she finished the race but was unhappy with her time of just under 45 minutes. She'd been too preoccupied with her living situation and memories and had not concentrated on her pace.

She milled about the race area, chatting with a few runners, but decided to head back to Marc's house. She wanted to shower and get into clean clothes before they went out to lunch.

Marc jumped out of bed shortly after Ravyn left. He couldn't fall back asleep.

He debated getting into his workout clothes and heading to the gym. But then he thought he'd surprise Ravyn by heading to her race and meeting her at the finish line.

He headed north on Peachtree toward the Brookhaven MARTA station. He hoped he wasn't too late and could find her in the crowd.

He found a parking spot and waited at the finish line among the crowd of other family members and friends, but never saw

Ravyn cross the finish line. He had no idea when she might cross, but after searching for nearly an hour, he decided to head back home.

Damn, the thought. I must have missed her. He returned to his BMW, but the line to exit was now crowded with exiting racers. Now he worried she'd get home before him and wonder where he was.

Ravyn drove south on Peachtree Road toward Marc's home but shot by the left turn she needed to make to turn toward his neighborhood. She was driving mindlessly, thinking about other things, and found herself heading toward her old condo building.

By the time she realized her driving mistake, she was close to Midtown and she was trying to figure out how to turn left and turn around. It wasn't easy. She was surprised at the amount of traffic on New Year's Day. Maybe all of these other drivers were headed to brunch or lunch or whatever.

If she were being honest with herself, Ravyn missed her old place. She'd had a one-bedroom, one-bath condo in Spire in Atlanta's Midtown. She'd lived there for many years, but her landlord, an investor who'd bought it at the bottom of the housing market, had decided to sell last year.

Although he'd offered Ravyn the first right to buy it, Ravyn didn't have the down payment, nor a way to pay the mortgage on the place. As her relationship with Marc had deepened, Marc asked her to move in with him. It seemed to solve her immediate housing problems.

But she was still feeling her way at his home. Most of what she'd been able to salvage of her belongings were stowed in his crowded detached garage.

Her belongings. She sighed as she thought about her possessions. Her sweaters, her blankets, her holiday decorations, her furniture. She'd rented another condo in her building for a short time and moved her belongings into a storage unit. She regretted that she'd never gotten insurance.

Ravyn turned left on 14th Street and then left again onto Piedmont Road. It put her very near Piedmont Park, a place she had loved to run to from her condo. Suddenly she was feeling very sad. She missed her old life. She loved Marc, but she missed her independence and freedom.

Ravyn pulled into Marc's short driveway at the front of his house, next to his older model BMW.

Marc's life had changed dramatically last year, too. He had sold a majority stake in his company, LindMark Enterprises. He could now certainly afford to upgrade his car, but he seemed to be comfortable in his old one. Ravyn thought he'd like a newer model with all the new technology and bells and whistles.

Although Marc had sold his company to Black Kat Investors for $3 million, keeping a minority interest, he'd owed his father almost a quarter of a million dollars, plus interest, and had a second mortgage on his house to pay off.

Ravyn understood why he kept his old car. It was paid off, just like her blue Honda Civic.

She unlocked the front door and called out. "I'm home!"

"How did the race go?" Marc asked, entering the living room, a kitchen towel in his hand. "I tried to meet you at the finish line, but I guessed I missed you."

"You did? At the Brookhaven MARTA station?"

"Yes. I wanted to surprise you."

"Well, I'm sorry I missed you," she said, kissing him. "That would have been a very nice surprise. I didn't run my best, though. Too much on my mind, I guess."

"What's on your mind?"

"I guess just the adjustments of living here and having a roommate."

Ravyn really didn't want to go into why she was feeling uncomfortable in Marc's house.

Marc looked a bit shocked. "Am I just a roommate to you?" Ravyn could see Marc tense up.

"Of course not. That's not what I meant."

"Well what did you mean?"

"I'm not used to living with anyone again. As a kid I shared a room with my sister Jane until we moved to a bigger house and we got our own rooms. I had a roommate in college and one when I got my first apartment."

"So, what are you saying?"

"That I'm getting used to living with someone again. You're a very cute someone I might add," Ravyn said, walking over to him, kissing him again, trying to put him at ease. "One I love and I love sleeping with. That's a roommate with benefits."

Ravyn could see Marc's shoulders begin to relax. "Marc, I just need some time getting used to this. Do you understand?"

"I guess I do. You know, I'm adjusting too. I'm not used to having so much stuff on the bathroom counter," he said.

Ravyn looked a bit sheepish. "I guess I do have a lot of products. Speaking of the bathroom, I'm going to jump in the shower and clean up before we go to lunch. You still want to go, don't you?"

"Yes. Need any help in there?" Marc asked, arching an eyebrow. "I can perform other benefits, you know."

"Well, I'm pretty sweaty all over."

"I can tell. But you smell kind of sexy."

"I might need some help getting my back clean."

"Just your back?"

"I might need some help with my front, too."

Standing close, Marc whispered, "As long as I can be of service."

Ravyn and Marc exited the walk-in shower in the bathroom, only to move to the bedroom. A long nap after making love, Ravyn and Marc realized their lunch was going to turn into a late lunch or early dinner. By the time they got ready to go to La Fonda Latina, which was close to the Garden Hills house, it was later than they expected and they had to wait for a table.

La Fonda was a fusion restaurant with Spanish, Mexican and Cuban items on the menu and Ravyn always loved getting the seafood paella, the *paella del mar*. It was loaded with scallops, calamari, salmon, mussels and shrimp. She asked Marc to split a double portion with her. Thankfully, Marc liked seafood as much as she did.

They ordered a bottle of light Spanish red wine to go with their meal.

"Oh, I'm stuffed. And there's enough to bring home for lunch at the office tomorrow," Ravyn said. "Unless you want to bring it for your lunch. Sorry. I just keep thinking about my lunches."

They paid their bill and Ravyn carried out the leftovers in a to-go box.

"It's OK," Marc said. "But you'll probably eat it before Monday. I wouldn't be surprised if you ate it for a midnight snack."

Ravyn sighed as they got in Marc's car. "Being on the pill really has its drawbacks. I didn't realize how much I'd want to eat before that time of the month."

"I'd tell you to go off the pill, but I kind of like not having to wear a condom. I feel more of a connection with you."

Ravyn smiled. "Yeah, it is better in that respect. But you might not want to make love to me if I gain a ton of weight."

"Ravyn, I'll love you no matter what."

"You say that now," she replied.

"No, I'll say that forever. Don't you forget it or doubt it."

Ravyn was silent for the short drive back to the house. She felt like she was always saying the wrong thing. Living together with Marc wasn't as easy, breezy as all the romance novels or movies made it seem. She could see it was going to take some work.

When they got back to the house, Ravyn put the leftovers in the refrigerator and broached the subject that she'd mulled over while she'd run the race earlier in the day.

"Marc, can we really discuss some renovations? To the house, I mean. We agreed on paint for the living room, but nothing else. Hell, half of my things are stuffed in your garage. I don't even have a picture hung on the wall."

"You want to hang pictures? Hang pictures. I haven't stopped you."

"But you aren't helping me with what I can or can't do."

"Well, hang whatever you want," Marc said, getting angry again. "I'm not going to dictate what you hang on the walls."

"But I want your input. I don't want to do it without you. You live here, too. I want to do it together."

"Where do you want to start?"

"I'd like to start with the living room, update the décor a bit. You know, new lamps and things. Then maybe some of the other rooms. Maybe we could go over to Home Goods near the house for ideas this weekend."

"Ravyn, I think you should go and pick out stuff like that. That's really not my thing."

Ravyn frowned. "Well, I want your input."

"You do not want my input. My input on home decor is boring. Just look at my place. I picked brown. You said it's boring brown. Even my mother says this place needs a woman's touch. It's yours to decorate. I'm sure I'll love whatever you pick."

She frowned again. "OK, but I'll save all my receipts, just in case you hate what I pick out."

"Honey, I'll only hate what you pick if it's bright pink with unicorns."

Ravyn laughed and hugged Marc close, looking up at his face, which was starting to sport a five o'clock shadow. She ruffled his brown hair. "I can't pick pink unicorns?"

"No."

"You're no fun. I hear pink unicorns are the hot new trend in home decoration this year."

"No pink unicorns."

Ravyn wandered the aisles of Home Goods in Buckhead, trying to decide what colors would work with the cream walls and Marc's dark brown leather couch. She was torn between gold and red accents and gold and yellow. In the end, she decided on gold and red.

As she'd promised, Ravyn had kept the receipts in case she didn't like the colors, or Marc didn't. She'd then gone to Target to check out some lamps. She didn't find any lamps she liked at Home Goods.

Marc had given her his credit card for her shopping spree for the house. That was kind of nice. She liked having to share expenses. Until now, she'd always had to make ends meet on her own, paying her condo rent, utilities and other housing bills. Now she and Marc were sharing those expenses.

Marc had wanted to keep paying the mortgage himself, but Ravyn had insisted on paying half, which was her share. Even paying just half the mortgage, she was paying about what she'd been paying for her condo.

Although Marc had taken out a second mortgage on his house, the sale of his company several months ago meant he was about to pay that off. Ravyn would have even less of her share to pay.

And by splitting utilities, she figured she would come out ahead in the end. She might even be able to have a real savings account.

Ravyn got home and dropped the Home Goods and Target bags on the couch. She wanted to see how the throw pillows looked and some of the other accents. She was nervous about the lamps she'd gotten at Target, selecting a kind of burgundy shade for the gold-toned lamp. They were kind of large, and she was hoping they wouldn't be too big for the end tables.

She took them out and placed them one way, then another on the end tables. She put the shades on and then placed the throw pillows on the couch. Ravyn looked this way and that, trying to decide if she liked them. Then she placed a throw blanket on the end of the leather couch. That was gold, and almost matched the gold-tone bases of the lamps.

Ravyn left the living room, then walked in again, trying to see it with new eyes. She wanted Marc's opinion, but he was at the gym. She was anxious for him to come home.

Ravyn was also excited to hang a couple of her pieces of artwork, such as they were. She had a nice watercolor of a blue heron she'd bought when she'd vacationed in St. Augustine, Florida, where she had happened upon an art show one Palm Sunday weekend.

Ravyn remembered walking up and down the streets of old St. Augustine, visiting the various artists' booths. The blue heron watercolor had caught her eye and she'd come back to that artist's booth twice before buying it.

She also had a nice framed print of a tiger, her college's mascot, in the snow in front of the University of Missouri's Jesse Hall. She liked that one because it reminded her of her time at college. She graduated in 2001 with a degree in journalism. She had gotten a job at the Atlanta daily paper after paying her dues for a few years at smaller newspapers in Georgia and Florida.

Ravyn smiled when she thought about hanging it next to Marc's University of Georgia bulldog framed poster, now that the University of Georgia and the University of Missouri were football rivals in the Southeastern Conference. Well, maybe not, she giggled inwardly. No reason to have another argument with Marc right away.

Ravyn found the hammer and a couple of nails and hung the blue heron watercolor on a blank wall in the hallway. She hung her Missouri tiger in the snow framed print on the opposite wall of Marc's Georgia bulldog print. He couldn't argue with that, could he?

She walked back into the living room, pleased with the new décor and color scheme. She liked the thought of curling up on the couch with Marc later that evening with a fire going in the fireplace and the warm throw blanket over her.

Ravyn texted Marc to see when he'd be home, then decided she'd get dinner started. She pulled out some chicken breasts from the refrigerator, an onion and reached for the garlic. She got a couple of potatoes out. She'd decided to roast those and sauté the chicken with the onions and garlic.

She pulled lettuce out for salad and got a can of black olives, a jar of marinated artichoke hearts and some blue cheese crumbles. Oil and vinegar, salt and pepper would round out the salad.

Finally, she pulled a bag of steamable broccoli florets out of the freezer. She'd start the broccoli in the microwave just about when dinner was ready.

Marc walked in the house only a few minutes after she'd gotten dinner started.

"Hey, it looks great in here," he called from the living room. "I like what you've done."

He walked into the kitchen, reaching from behind to give Ravyn a hug.

"Whew! You need a shower."

"I've started this great boxing class at the gym. It's a great workout. And I got to spar with the instructor a bit."

"Boxing? Is this a new class?"

"Yeah. They are offering it in the new year. I'm glad I signed up early. There is a wait list now. Will dinner wait for me?"

"Yes. The potatoes won't be ready for another 30 minutes. We'll have broccoli, too."

"OK. I'll jump in the shower and be out in 10."

"Take your time. I'll open a bottle of pinot noir and it will be ready when you come out."

"You're perfect. Love you." Marc turned Ravyn to face him and kissed her deeply.

"Love you, too," she said, wrinkling her nose. "Now go get cleaned up."

When Marc emerged about 15 minutes later, he wore gray sweatpants and a red and black flannel shirt. His wavy brown hair was damp and slightly ruffled.

"Hey sexy," Ravyn said as he came down the hallway and walked into the kitchen.

"Hey sexy yourself."

Ravyn handed a glass of the red wine to Marc. "Dinner will be ready in just a few minutes."

"Wish it was an hour."

"It won't wait for an hour. Everything will burn if we wait an hour. But maybe we can discuss waiting until after dessert."

"Dessert?" Marc raised an eyebrow and smiled.

Chapter 2

Marc was nervous as he walked up and down the jewelry cases at Tiffany & Co.'s jewelry store in Phipps Plaza, a tony shopping mall in Buckhead. He was waiting for Ravyn's best friend, Julie Montgomery, to arrive.

He had no idea what kind of engagement ring he wanted to buy for Ravyn, or what kind of cut she would like. There were so many choices! Why wasn't Julie here? he wondered, as he stalked the cases one more time.

Marc could tell the clerk was getting exasperated with him.

"I'm just waiting on my girlfriend's best friend," he explained again.

"Very good, sir," the clerk said.

"I'm sorry I'm late," Julie said, rushing through the doors at Tiffany's and coming to a stop, staring around her. "This is awesome! I can't believe you are going to pop the question!"

"I brought the ring you suggested," he said, pulling a small white gold ring out of his pocket.

"You brought it with you? Ravyn loves that ring! I've never seen her not wear it. What did you say when you took it?"

"I didn't tell her. I just took it. Do you think she'll miss it?"

"Oh God. She'll tear the house down looking for it! Why didn't you just take a photo with your phone?"

"Then how would I know what size ring she wears?"

13

"Silly, you just run a pen around the inside of the ring on a piece of paper."

"Oh, I didn't think of that."

Julie rolled her eyes. Dear God, he's cute, but he's dense sometimes, she thought. I hope Ravyn knows what she's getting into.

"Well, let's look at what you think she might like," Julie said.

"Oh. I don't know what she'd like. I thought *you* would. That's why I asked you to meet me here."

Julie tried to keep from rolling her eyes again.

"Well, let's look at the ring, since you have it," Julie said, taking the ring from Marc. "These are marquise cut gems, with tiny diamonds on the side."

"It is?"

"Yes, these three sapphires are a marquise cut, sir," the clerk said, pointing to the small ring and trying to be helpful.

"Have you seen any other rings she wears?" Julie asked.

"I think she has another ring like this. There are three blue stones, but they are a little bigger than the ones on this ring. That's a sapphire right?"

"Yes, sir. Blue gems are generally sapphires," the clerk said, trying not to sound condescending.

Marc blew out an angry breath. He was not liking the clerk. And he didn't want to end up giving him a high commission.

"Maybe we should come back," Marc said to Julie.

"No, no, sir," the clerk said, realizing he might have given offense. "I apologize if I have been unhelpful. We have some lovely marquise cut diamonds right over here." He pointed to an engagement ring case. "But we also have some other cuts. There is the oval cut, which looks similar. The emerald cut is very popular too. And we have the round cut and princess cut, which are also very popular."

Marc sighed. All of this jewelry was overwhelming. The first time he'd gotten married, his future wife had picked out what she wanted. He was beginning to think he didn't want to surprise Ravyn with the ring and just let her do the same. Let her come back to Tiffany's and pick out what she wanted.

"Of course, if your future fiancée changes her mind and doesn't care for the ring, we can change it," the clerk said.

"You may have to. I have no idea what she'd like," Marc said, rather bitterly.

"No, no!" Julie said, adamantly. "I really think she'd like a marquise cut, or something close to it. Look at what she already has. She's bought those because she likes them. But do you want a diamond or do you want to give her a sapphire? You know she loves those."

"Madam, a diamond is an engagement ring," the clerk started to say, trying to cut Julie off.

"Well, if a sapphire engagement ring was good enough for Princess Diana, it should be good enough for Ravyn," Julie said sharply. "Don't you agree?"

The clerk hesitated. Princess Diana? Why was this woman obsessed with sapphires? "Yes, madam," the clerk said. "But we would have to custom order a sapphire in that cut. When do you need the ring by?"

"I'm proposing on Valentine's Day," Marc said.

"We may not be able to guarantee that, but we do have some lovely pear-shaped diamonds. Then perhaps you could choose one of our sapphire and diamond wedding bands. That way we could have that for you by Valentine's Day," the clerk said.

"Let's try to see if we can get the ring Ravyn will love," Julie said.

Marc let out another big breath. "I have no idea."

Julie and the clerk locked eyes. Julie could tell that they would be rivals for what Marc would buy.

"Marc, you know Ravyn loves sapphires. She adores them. Hell, she named her blue Honda Civic sapphire. So, start with a sapphire."

The clerk drew in a breath. If a woman named her car sapphire, he was doubting he would sell a high-priced diamond solitaire today.

"This pear-shaped diamond is truly exquisite. And here, we have some lovely wedding band sets," the clerk said, pointing to the glass display case. He unlocked one with his key and pulled out the sapphire and diamond sets. "As I said, we have this lovely diamond and sapphire band. That would satisfy the desire for sapphires."

He held up the ring and placed it in Marc's palm.

"That might be nice," Julie said, peering over his shoulder.

"And I suggest a platinum setting for the engagement ring and the wedding band," the clerk said. "You really want the best for your future fiancée."

Julie smirked at the clerk. "Well what about a nice white gold setting? Just as good as platinum."

"Not just as good as platinum, madam."

"Well, it was good enough for my engagement ring, and I've been married for almost 15 years," Julie said, angrily.

Marc looked to Julie and the clerk, perplexed. He felt like he was out of his league and there was a war about to brew in the high-end jewelry store.

"Yes, madam. We have white gold settings, but I recommend a platinum setting," the clerk said.

"OK," Marc said, putting up his hand. "I want the pear-shaped diamond in a platinum setting and the sapphire and diamond wedding band for Ravyn. I'll just take the plain wedding band for me. Can you do that?"

"Yes, sir. I can have that right away," the clerk said. "I can mark it a rush, but that will cost extra."

"That's fine. I want the engagement ring by Valentine's Day," Marc said. "Can I put a hold on the wedding bands?"

"Yes, sir," the clerk smiled. "We'd just need a deposit."

Julie smiled. Marc seemed to have some balls after all.

"Let me size the ring you brought with you. She wears this on her ring finger, correct?"

"Yes, she does."

"And let me clean this ring for you as well. Oils can build up and make it look dull. We want it to sparkle. Let's just step over here and discuss the payment of the rings," the clerk said.

When the engagement ring finally arrived, Marc went back to Tiffany's to pick it up. He carried that small robin egg blue ring box in his pocket like it was kryptonite. He didn't want to leave it anywhere where Ravyn might find it. He'd left it in the bottom of his gym bag, then moved it to a secret spot in the detached garage, and then into a dress shoe in his closet.

Marc planned to ask Ravyn to marry him on Valentine's Day, well before her self-imposed Ides of March deadline when she could walk away from him free and clear.

Ravyn had called it a trial cohabitation, the opposite of a trial separation. She wanted to give their living together three months. If by mid-March she was unhappy or wanted to move out to her own place, she would. Marc had reluctantly agreed to the deal. What choice did he have?

The thought of Ravyn leaving terrified Marc. Essentially, he was trying to preempt Ravyn's decision to leave. He didn't want to lose her. He'd lost her once and he wasn't about to lose her again.

Ravyn and Marc had met almost two years before, when he was CEO of LindMark Enterprises and Ravyn was a freelance writer doing a profile story on him for Atlanta Trend magazine.

Ravyn wrote the profile piece and sparks had flown, first the angry kind, then the passionate kind. She eventually began working for Marc to help with marketing and public relations and their work relationship quickly heated, turning them into a couple.

17

But Marc's former public relations agent and former girlfriend Laura Lucas had other ideas about the pair and actively worked to come between them.

Laura sabotaged Marc's company by breaking into his computer and corrupting his fourth-quarter financial report.

Marc didn't realize Laura's deception and blamed Ravyn for the incorrect financial report that he sent to prospective investors. By the time he'd realized what Laura had done, he and Ravyn had broken up.

They attempted a reconciliation but it didn't last. Marc realized too late he didn't want to let Ravyn go.

Ravyn, however, had moved on and tried online dating. Marc, in turn, created a fake profile using his brother's photo. With the help of Ravyn's best friend Julie, Marc was matched with Ravyn's profile.

It took time, but Marc won her over. Ravyn moved into his small three-bedroom, two-bath bungalow in the Garden Hills area of Buckhead, a posh neighborhood of Atlanta in December.

Ravyn ran the Atlanta Track Club's Hearts and Soles 5K Feb. 6. She'd tried to talk Marc into doing the race with her. They could do it as a couple and in costume, but Marc had flatly refused. He was a gym rat, not a road runner. He preferred a quick 30 minutes on the treadmill over asphalt.

"We could just walk it then," Ravyn implored.

"You'll have to let me sit this one out," he replied. "I'll go to the gym while you do the race."

Ravyn was disappointed but asked her friend Angela to do the best costume contest with her. They didn't win, but had fun running the race, coming up with a pink and red Valentine-themed costume that wasn't too clumsy to run in. Angela had found pink tutus and Ravyn felt sure they'd wear them again at next year's race.

Ravyn returned home mid-morning but Marc wasn't there. Ravyn could sense that something was off about Marc. He'd been moody, quiet. She couldn't put her finger on it, but he seemed withdrawn.

In the past few months, she would have chalked it up to the stress he felt about selling the majority interest in LindMark Enterprises. He'd built that company from nothing and now Kyle Quitman and Black Kat Investors owned 75 percent of it.

Marc had stayed on at the company, basically running it just as he always did. Marc thought he'd been kept on as a consultant, but Quitman had other ideas.

Quitman bought and sold companies. He didn't run them. Although, Quitman had an office in LindMark's small office in Midtown's Colony Square building.

Ravyn had met Quitman in December. He seemed nice enough, and he and Marc seemed to get along.

Ravyn's work life had taken a turn, too. Her former boss and editor, Jennifer Bagley, had been transferred to a sister magazine in Dallas, making Ravyn's life at *Cleopatra* magazine much better.

Ravyn was managing editor for *Cleopatra*, a lifestyle magazine in Atlanta, but she and Jennifer had never really become friendly in the office. When Jennifer and Ad Director Joel Greenberg had gotten caught in a compromising sexual relationship at the office, Jennifer, rather than Joel, had been transferred.

Horizon Publications, the New York-based company that owned several magazines across the country, had a no nepotism rule, and Ravyn could see the powers that be took the rule seriously.

Ravyn and Jennifer actually seemed to have a better working relationship with several states between them. They chatted on the phone often and wrote a flurry of emails every day to keep deadlines on track. Ravyn could breathe a sigh of relief without Jennifer just down the hall or popping in to Ravyn's office unannounced.

Joel, however, had moped around the office ever since Jennifer left for Dallas. Joel had confided to Ravyn he'd been in love with Jennifer and didn't want her to leave Atlanta.

Jennifer had confided to Ravyn she wasn't sure she'd stay in Dallas or with Horizon, but she was ambiguous about her feelings for Joel. Ravyn hadn't heard any gossip that Jennifer was quitting. Maybe Jennifer was planning to stay in Dallas. Maybe she was making a life for herself there.

Some of Ravyn's coworkers created an office pool to place bets on when Joel would start dating again. Ravyn thought that was a bit crass and heartless. Joel really did seem to miss Jennifer. She thought he was more invested in their relationship. She had no idea if Jennifer was still pining for Joel, but he certainly was acting like a heart-sick teenager.

Ravyn passed Joel in the hall three days before Valentine's Day.

"Hey, Joel. How are you doing?" she asked him.

"Not good. I was hoping to fly down to Dallas to see Jennifer for Valentine's this weekend, but she says she's too busy," Joel said, sighing deeply.

"Well, can you go down next weekend?" Ravyn asked.

"I think she's giving me the brush off," Joel said. "I think she might be seeing someone else."

"This soon? Surely not."

"She's a beautiful woman, Ravyn. And I'm a washed up old man."

"Joel, don't say that. You're not an old man."

"Ravyn, I'm about 15 years older than her and about 25 years older than you. She's found someone young and handsome in Dallas."

"I'm sure that's not what's happened."

Joel gave Ravyn a withering look. Ravyn knew he had more life wisdom and probably knew what he was talking about when it came to Jennifer.

Marc was pacing the floor in the kitchen, waiting for Ravyn to come home Friday evening ahead of Valentine's weekend. Valentine's Day was on Sunday and he'd made reservations for Atlanta Fish Market, a Buckhead restaurant they both enjoyed.

He was very nervous about Sunday since he planned to propose to Ravyn. He'd called the restaurant ahead and let them know his plans and ordered champagne for the table.

Ravyn got home Friday, surprised to find Marc's car in the driveway. She usually got home before him, even with the longer commute up Peachtree Road.

"You're home early," she said. "Everything OK?"

"Fine. Just took off a little early today."

"Did you go to the gym?"

"No. I'll go tomorrow morning. Will you go for a run tomorrow?"

"Yeah. I've got a good route around the neighborhood now. I've mapped out a 3-mile run."

"Just be careful."

"I will. What's for dinner? Did you start something?

"I thought I'd just grill some chicken tonight."

"On the gas grill?"

"Yeah."

"Isn't it too cold out there?"

"Well, I won't be standing out there once I put the chicken on. I'll be in the house. But I'll time it."

"Better you than me. Too cold for my blood."

"Well, I can warm you up if you need it. And we can start a fire tonight."

"I honestly love that we can start a fire in the fireplace. I always wished my condo had had a fireplace. Makes me almost love winter. Almost."

Marc moved toward Ravyn. "I'd love to make love to you in front of the fireplace."

"You need a bear skin rug to do that, don't you? I'll need to go back to Home Goods to see if I can find that," Ravyn said, smiling up at him.

"I'm not sure they carry a bear skin rug."

"I'm not sure they carry it, either."

"What if we pull that small rug near the door over?"

"I swear I'll find a towel before I make love on that rug by the door. That's got to be full of mud and dirt," Ravyn said, thoroughly disgusted.

"Ok, Ok. I was just trying to be romantic."

"Not with that rug you aren't. I'll find something. Something clean."

"OK, I need to get dinner started," Marc said. "What do you want with the chicken?"

"What about some rice and I'll do some Brussels sprouts."

"Sounds great. Then we can think about the fireplace," he said.

Marc and Ravyn finished up dinner and loaded the dishwasher with their few plates. Ravyn had found a clean, plush towel and placed it in front of the gas fireplace, which Marc had lit.

They started to get glasses of wine to take into the living room as Ravyn's cat Felix came winding his way around the both of them. He chirped several times before he settled himself on the towel Ravyn had just placed in front of the warm fireplace.

"Felix!"

"Kick him off the towel," Marc said, irritated that the cat got the spot he'd intended for other activities.

"Let me grab that quilt off the guest bed. It's bigger anyway."

Ravyn returned and put the blue and white quilt down on the hardwood floor. Marc pulled Ravyn closer, kissing her deeply. Ravyn moved under his body and felt him pulling her long-sleeved T-shirt up over her head. She pulled his polo shirt off, too.

Marc undid Ravyn's bra and a shiver ran over her skin as Marc's warm breath moved across her nipple. He sucked it gently, slowly, then moved to the other nipple.

Ravyn's breath caught in the back of her throat, almost a gasp. Before long, they were both naked in front of the fireplace. Although Ravyn felt a chill, she could feel the warmth of the fireplace on the side facing her body. Marc kept kissing Ravyn, moving down her body, which sent a very different kind of chill down her.

Ravyn moaned when Marc got to the sweet spot between her legs. She loved that he liked to give oral sex, making sure she was satisfied. As he worked his magic tongue over her, she gasped before she bucked her hips as she reached climax. An orgasm electrified her whole being.

Marc then moved over Ravyn, easing himself into her. "Are you ready for me?" Marc asked, his voice husky.

"Yes, baby. I'm ready. I want you."

"Oh, God, I want you too."

Ravyn began to feel herself aroused again, even though she had just had an orgasm. She moaned again, feeling the rise of ecstasy in her body.

Marc pushed into Ravyn, sweat starting to glisten off his forearms. Ravyn could feel the soft texture of the quilt beneath her with Marc's every thrust.

"Oh, God! Ravyn!" Marc called out before he collapsed on top of her.

Marc and Ravyn awoke later, entangled in the quilt, as the fire danced on the gas logs. Marc rolled over and groaned, not enjoying the quilt on the hard floor, which offered no support for his middle-aged bones.

Ravyn rolled over too, feeling the stiffness in her legs and the soreness between them.

"We need to move to the bedroom," Marc said. "Or at least I need to. I need a soft landing."

"Yeah, I do, too. We need to get a memory foam rug or mat, if we are going to do this again."

"Well, I'd like to do this again, but not unless we have something softer. My bones can't take this."

"Bedroom," Ravyn said, hauling herself off the floor.

Marc turned the gas fireplace off and they moved to the back of the house.

Ravyn flopped on the queen bed, with Marc joining her shortly thereafter.

"I love you so," he said.

"I love you, too."

Ravyn rolled to face Marc in the bed. "Are you going to sleep?"

"Maybe. Are you ready for bed?"

"Not really."

"What do you have in mind?

"I think we could cuddle."

"I'd like that."

Ravyn rolled over, curling into Marc's body. They fell asleep with their arms wrapped around each other.

Chapter 3

Marc was trying not to look or feel nervous as he and Ravyn drove north on Peachtree Road toward Atlanta Fish Market in Buckhead for their Valentine's dinner. He was glad for the heated seats in his old BMW. It was cold that evening.

Marc had Ravyn's engagement ring in the breast pocket of his sports coat. He felt like the ring box was burning a hole in it. He'd opted not to wear an outer coat, hence his gratitude for the heated seats. Ravyn had wrapped herself up in her winter coat and wore her lined leather gloves.

Marc turned right on Pharr Road, then pulled into the front of the restaurant, stopping for the valet service. He'd started around to open Ravyn's car door, but another valet had opened it and held out his hand for her, helping her out of the BMW.

Marc had gotten around at least to take Ravyn's arm and head to the front door of the restaurant. As they walked in, there was a large aquarium to the left, near the hostess stand. The restaurant was crowded. Couples sat on the benches and also had been standing outside on the short landing of the restaurant under a couple of tall heat lamps.

They were a little early for their reservation, Marc knew, and he felt sure they'd have to wait. The pair queued up to the hostess stand to give their names.

"Linder, two for dinner," Marc said, holding up two fingers.

"Yes, Mr. Linder," the hostess said. "We have your reservation at 8, but we're running a little behind. It will probably be 30 minutes after your reservation time. You are welcome to wait at the bar and we'll come get you when your table is ready."

"Thank you," he said. He turned to Ravyn. "Would you care for a glass of wine?"

"That would be great," she said, taking off her gloves and blowing on her hands. "It will help warm me up."

"So, a red then?"

"Yes. A cab, I think."

Marc steered her toward the bar and ordered two glasses of Cabernet Sauvignon. He handed over his credit card and he took the first glass, giving it to Ravyn. He took a rather large gulp of his own glass.

Ravyn watched Marc as she sipped her wine. "Everything OK?" she asked.

"Fine. I'm fine. Just wish we could start dinner. It smells good in here, doesn't it?"

"It does. Do you know what you're getting tonight?"

"I'd like some oysters to start."

"That sounds good. Should we walk over and see what kind they have tonight?"

Atlanta Fish Market has a large glass display case with all kinds of fish on ice. They could see red snapper, salmon, scallops and other aquatic delicacies. Ravyn could feel her mouth water. It all looked good.

Marc began to nurse his wine, as Ravyn was doing. He didn't want to drink it too fast and have it go to his head. He needed to keep his wits about him and remember the words he wanted to say tonight. He was planning to propose over dessert and had ordered glasses of champagne delivered to the table as dessert arrived.

As the pair finished their wine, the hostess came over and told them their table was ready. They headed up to the upper level to a small table. Marc helped Ravyn into her chair, then seated himself across from her.

"This is very romantic," Ravyn said, peering over the railing.

"Of course. I just wanted Valentine's Day to be special for you."

When the waiter arrived, they ordered a half dozen oysters and the calamari appetizer. Calamari was one of Ravyn's favorites. She'd often made it her meal when she came to the restaurant for lunch.

They continued to look over the menu for their entrees.

"Are you going to have lobster tonight? It is a special occasion," Marc said.

"I really think I want rainbow trout. It looked so good in the display."

"That looks good, too."

"Are you getting the lobster?"

"I'm thinking I'll get my usual. I really like their filet mignon."

"Oh, I remember you liked that when we came years ago."

"I like mine medium rare and they do it just right."

Their oysters arrived with the calamari right behind.

"Are you ready to order?" the waiter asked.

"Ravyn, after you."

Ravyn ordered the trout and a glass of pinot grigio. Marc ordered his steak and a side of steamed broccoli. He ordered another glass of the cabernet.

"I'm going to sleep well tonight with the steak and red wine," Marc said.

"I can drive home if you need to nap after this meal," Ravyn teased.

"I think I can manage," Marc smiled.

They talked about the week ahead. Ravyn had the April section of *Cleopatra* magazine to get started. That meant assigning out stories to freelancers and making sure she was within the monthly budget.

Marc had money on his mind, too. He planned to crunch first quarter numbers at LindMark Enterprises, hoping they would be in the positive range. Then he'd make projections for the second quarter.

He'd sold his company at the start of the fourth quarter of 2015 and wanted to provide solid numbers and a profit to show Black Kat Investors it hadn't made a mistake with the purchase.

An hour later, they finished their meals and the waiter began to clear their plates, asking if they'd like to box the rest of their meals.

Marc shook his head no, but Ravyn nodded yes, since she had about half of her trout left. The waiter then returned with Ravyn's meal in a small bag and presented the dessert menu.

Ravyn held up her hand. "I don't think I could eat another bite," she said, trying to wave off the dessert menu. But the waiter looked at Marc, who nodded, and placed the menu in front of her.

"Come on, Ravyn," Marc cajoled. "We can split something, right?"

"Marc, you hardly ever want dessert."

"Well, this is Valentine's Day," he said, looking over the dessert menu.

"We have a special dessert tonight," the waiter said. "We have a half dozen chocolate covered strawberries."

"Oh, I think I could do that," Ravyn laughed. "It's not really dessert if it's fruit, right?"

"Very good, madam," the waiter said. He looked at Marc, who gave another slight nod.

Ravyn raised an eyebrow. What was going on?

"Ravyn, you know I love you," Marc said, his voice a little shaky.

"And I love you," she said slowly.

Marc moved to the side of the table, getting down on his knee and reaching for the Tiffany ring box in his jacket.

Ravyn's eyes got wide when she realized what was happening. "Oh, Marc! Oh my God, Marc!" Her eyes began to water.

"Ravyn, my life was empty without you. Empty. I came alive when I was with you. And then I lost you. I don't want to ever be without you again. I will spend the rest of my life trying to make you happy. Will you do me the honor of being my wife?"

Ravyn could feel her eyes fill with tears. She could only shake her head and whisper, "Yes."

Tables around them began to clap and whistle. Several men came over and clapped Marc on the back after he stood up to hug Ravyn. He placed the ring on the third finger of her left hand and she stared at it.

The waiter appeared with their strawberries and a bottle of champagne. He opened it with a deft "pop" and poured out two glasses. Patrons began clapping and cheering louder.

Marc grinned from ear to ear but was trying not to get choked up. Ravyn dabbed her eyes with her napkin. She kept looking at her hand, in disbelief. She was engaged!

"Oh, Marc. It's perfect!" she said, turning her hand to catch the light on the ring.

"Julie helped me pick it out."

"Julie knew before me?"

"It was supposed to be a surprise."

"Well, it certainly was."

"Do you like the ring? We can exchange it if you want."

"No, it's perfect. Absolutely perfect."

Ravyn and Marc clinked their champagne flutes. As she tilted the glass toward her mouth, she side eyed her ring.

"I guess I'm going to have some news for the office tomorrow."

"I guess you will."

"I'm going to have to call my parents tonight, and my sister, and Julie," Ravyn said.

"I guess I should call my mother, too."

"Of course, you should call her."

"We can do that later. Let's just enjoy dessert and the champagne."

Ravyn took a bite of one of the chocolate-covered strawberries, its sweet juice beginning to run down the side of her mouth. She quickly wiped her mouth and took another sip of champagne.

"Oh my gosh, these are good. I wonder where they got them."

Marc took one and bit in as well. "They are good."

Ravyn bit into a second strawberry, severing it in half. She then finished it, placing the green top on the plate between them.

"Go ahead and finish them," Marc said.

"I might want to box the rest," she said. "But I am going to finish the champagne."

Marc signaled the waiter, asking for a box for the remaining strawberries and requesting the bill.

As they stood outside waiting for his car, he held Ravyn close. He felt lighter, like he could take on the world at that very moment. With Ravyn by his side, he felt invincible.

When they got home, Ravyn immediately got on the phone to her parents.

"Mom, I have some news. Is dad there too?"

"Oh, Ravyn, did Marc propose tonight?"

"How did you know?"

"Well, Marc called your father a couple of weeks ago to ask for your hand, honey," Ravyn's mother, Kaye, said. "He said he planned to do it on Valentine's Day. And today's Valentine's Day."

"So, you knew before me?"

"He said he wanted it to be a surprise. Were you surprised?"

"I was. We had a nice dinner at a fancy Buckhead restaurant and he proposed over dessert, with chocolate-covered strawberries and champagne. The good stuff. Mom, he got down on his knee."

"Is the ring pretty?"

"It's gorgeous. I'll send you a picture of it."

"Hi darling," Ravyn's father, John, interrupted. "Did Marc make it official?"

"He did."

"Are you happy, honey?"

"I am."

"That's all that matters," her father said. "I'll put your mother back on."

Ravyn and her mother chatted a bit more. Kaye asked if they knew what their wedding date might be.

"Oh, Mom, we haven't gotten that far yet."

"You just let us know."

"Of course, I will."

"And send me a picture of that ring."

"I will."

"I'm so happy for you, Ravyn."

"Thanks, Mom. I'm happy, too."

Ravyn next called her sister, Jane, letting her know of her engagement. Jane shrieked with excitement. "I'm so happy for you! I want a picture of the ring. When are you getting married? Oh, this is so exciting! I was hoping Marc would ask you to marry him. You two seem so good together."

Jane was talking so fast, Ravyn could barely get a word in, or answer her questions. Again, she told her sister that they hadn't set a date. That would come later. But Ravyn did have a question for her sister. "Jane, will you be my maid of honor? Or I guess it's my matron of honor since you are married."

Jane began to cry. "I'd love to be your matron of honor! But you don't have to ask me because you were my maid of honor."

"No, Jane, I want you by my side for the wedding," Ravyn said. She could feel herself tearing up as well. "You are my sister. My best friend. Of course, I want you at my wedding."

By the time she called Julie, Ravyn was feeling emotionally drained. Who knew engagements could be so taxing?

"Do you like the ring?" Julie asked. "Do you like the diamond? We debated getting you a sapphire."

"No, I love the diamond. It's so sparkly! It's perfect."

"I think so, too."

"Thanks for helping Marc pick it out."

"Did he tell you he took one of your rings to the store? The one you wear all the time?"

"He didn't tell me that! I think I know the day he did it, though. But I wore a sterling silver ring that day."

"I was sure you'd figure out it was missing. I kind of yelled at him about taking it. But I'm glad he had it, so we knew your size right away. I wanted you to get a good ring. One that suits you. And he got a good ring. I mean, Tiffany's!"

"It does suit me. He did really well in picking it out, but I guess I have you to thank for that. I just can't believe you didn't give me a hint at all. I mean, you could have let me know so I wasn't so shocked. I had no idea this was coming."

"Then it wouldn't have been a surprise, now would it? I want to know exactly how he proposed. Every detail. Don't leave anything out."

Ravyn recounted the dinner, what they each ordered, and dessert with the chocolate-covered strawberries and champagne, and how Marc proposed. "Julie, he got down on his knee! I thought they only did that in the movies."

"So, he did it right. Are you happy, Ravyn?"

"I'm delirious. But really, I can't believe this is happening. It's a little overwhelming. I mean, I'm getting married!"

"So where is your future husband? What is Marc doing now?"

"My future husband? That seems strange to say. He was going to call his mother, but I think they are off the phone now. I'm not sure if I'm supposed to call her tonight or not."

"Call her tomorrow. Don't get too tired. You need some engagement sex tonight."

"What?"

"Listen, when I got engaged to Rob it was one of the best nights of sex I've ever had."

"Not sure that I needed to know that."

"Hey, right now, he's happy. You're happy. Get off the phone with me and go make each other happy."

Ravyn laughed. "OK, if you insist."

"Oh, I insist."

Ravyn walked back to the master bedroom, where Marc was laying on the bed.

"You OK?" she asked.

"I just ate a lot of that steak, and it was pretty big. I'm feeling very full."

"Me, too. But Julie says we need to have engagement sex."

"Julie said what?" Marc said, trying to sit up. He fell back on the bed. "Engagement sex? Is that a thing?"

"I'm not really sure," she said, sitting on the edge of the bed and beginning to undress, unzipping the eggplant-colored A-line dress she had worn that evening.

"Let me help you with that," Marc said, sitting up properly and helping pull down the zipper all the way. He lifted her light brown hair and kissed the nape of her neck.

Ravyn gave a little growl in her throat. Marc pulled the dress down from her shoulders and unhooked her bra, then cupped her breasts.

"You are so beautiful. How did I get so lucky?" he whispered in her neck, working his hands over her nipples. Ravyn felt them get erect.

Ravyn stood up and stepped out of her dress, letting it and her bra slip to the floor. She then slipped her cornflower blue-colored thong down, the one with a bow in the front, and let it fall to the floor as well.

Marc raised an eyebrow. "A thong? You hate those things. What do you call them? Butt floss?"

"They are uncomfortable. I don't like them, but I was hoping I was having Valentine's sex tonight. I didn't know I would get Valentine's sex *and* engagement sex. It's like a two-fer."

Ravyn arched her eyebrow again. "And you, sir, are very overdressed."

Marc stood up and did a little mock strip tease, pulling off his shirt and his pants, then slipped off his plaid boxers with a silly flourish.

Ravyn could see he was already aroused, his penis erect. She admired his body. Marc was lean and kept himself trim with all of his work outs at the gym.

Marc was a self-described gym rat. But Ravyn could also see he had just a little bit of a belly now, a sign of getting older. She smiled at him.

"What's that smile for?"

"Come closer and you'll find out."

Ravyn reached for him and began to stroke his erection. They fell back onto the bed, Ravyn giving his shaft a little tug. Then she ran her nail over the tip of his penis.

"Hey, that's sensitive territory," Marc exclaimed.

"I'll be careful."

"You'd better be or there will be no engagement sex," he teased.

Marc rolled on top of Ravyn, kissing her, then her breasts. He started to work down her stomach, intending to find the pleasure spot between her legs.

"Oh, God," Ravyn exclaimed. Then Ravyn pulled on his arms. "Marc, no. Come in me now. I want you now. I want us to come together."

Marc entered her, their breathing becoming rapid and heavy. Their sex was impatient, hurried. Marc thrust in Ravyn, who climaxed quickly. Marc was not far behind. He fell on top of her, Ravyn wrapping her arms around him and holding him tightly. She could feel herself beginning to cry, not from unhappiness, but from ecstasy.

"Are you OK? Did I hurt you?" Marc asked quietly, stroking the tears away from her cheeks. "I didn't want to hurt you. I never want to hurt you."

"No, I'm fine. I'm just overwhelmed," she said, wiping her own eyes. "I really didn't know I could be so happy."

"I'm happy, too. I love you so much, sometimes it scares me. Without you I feel like I can't breathe."

Ravyn rolled over onto her left elbow, reaching for Marc and stroking his damp hair. "I know. I feel that way, too. In some ways I feel like I hardly know you and in other ways I feel like I've known you forever. Like I've always known you."

"I feel the same way." Marc pulled Ravyn to him. "Ravyn, Ravyn. I don't want this feeling to ever end."

Chapter 4

Ravyn woke up Monday and wondered if Valentine's Day night had been a dream. But she looked over on the nightstand and saw her engagement ring in a small bowl she used to hold her other rings.

Marc stirred beside her. "Good morning, fiancée."

"Good morning, fiancé." Ravyn giggled. "That sounds weird to say."

Marc kissed Ravyn, wrapping his arms around her. "I love you, fiancée."

Ravyn smiled. "That has a nice ring to it. Speaking of rings, I really love what you picked out."

"I'm glad, but you really do have Julie to thank for that. She seemed to know what you liked. She gave it her seal of approval, but the clerk said you could exchange it," Marc smiled.

"No, it's perfect. I keep telling you that, but it is. I just love it."

"You'll wear it to work today?"

"Of course! Why wouldn't I?"

"I don't know. I don't know how women do these things."

"Well, I'm wearing it to work today and every day from now on. I will only take it off when I shower and sleep."

"We should probably get it insured, just in case."

"Oh, Marc, I hope it wasn't too expensive."

"Never too expensive for your engagement ring, Ravyn."

"Now you're making me nervous to wear it."

"Don't be silly. We'll just call the insurance company to insure it. Better safe than sorry. I think I can do it through my homeowner's insurance."

"Call today. I've learned my lesson about not having insurance, that's for sure."

Ravyn smiled as she drove to work. She smiled that Julie was right. Engagement sex was incredible. She smiled because she was excited to share her news with her co-workers.

Ravyn was still a bit bewildered that she was an engaged woman, but she kept looking at the ring finger on her left hand and the pear-cut diamond on it.

As she pulled into the parking deck of her office building, she got nervous about what she would say. Would she just go about her morning and wait for someone to notice? With Jennifer Bagley now at the magazine in Dallas, she wasn't sure anyone *would* notice.

Ravyn was friendly with the other women in her office, the saleswomen, office manager and other administrative personnel, but she primarily worked closely with men there: Ad Director Joel Greenberg, Art Director Chase Riley and staff photographer Gavin Owens.

She was sure the men wouldn't notice. She thought then she might go all day waiting for someone to notice her engagement ring and for her to share her news.

Ravyn stepped off the elevator and went to her office. After putting down her purse and the cloth bag she used to pack her lunch and manila folders that held paperwork from the weekend, she walked to the break room to get coffee.

Joel Greenberg, wearing his usual sweater vest, stood at the coffee station, pouring out dark brown coffee.

"Want some?" he asked.

"Yes. Let me get my mug," she said, reaching into the upper cabinet for her cup.

"Hey, what's that?"

"What's what?"

"Is that an engagement ring?"

"Oh, you noticed!"

"Noticed? It practically blinded me," Joel smiled. "Congratulations, Ravyn."

"Thanks. Marc proposed last night on Valentine's Day."

"Romantic."

"It was. How was your Valentine's? Did you talk to Jennifer?"

"Ah, I think we're breaking up, actually."

"Oh, Joel. I'm sorry. I know you cared for her."

"Well, she's apparently met someone else in Dallas. I think she's planning to sell her house here in Atlanta and move there permanently."

"That seems quick," Ravyn said. "I mean her meeting someone else. She told you that?"

"Not in so many words, but she's grown distant. She hasn't called or FaceTimed me in over a week. When she first moved in January, we talked or used FaceTime almost every day. She said she really didn't like it there."

"Is she just busy with work?"

"I think she's just moved on. I guess I'll have to as well."

"I am sorry, Joel."

"Hey, don't worry about me. Jennifer was probably out of my league anyway."

"What do you mean, out of your league?"

"She was probably too young for me. I'm 60 this year."

"And?"

"And she was just 45 — not even. She turns 45 this year."

"I don't think that's a wide enough age difference. You weren't robbing the cradle, Joel. If she was in her 20s, I'd have been worried about you."

"Well, maybe I should find myself a nice 25 year old to make me forget about Jennifer."

Ravyn tried not to involuntarily shudder. She gave Joel a weak smile. "Maybe she's just been busy."

"Yeah, busy with someone else."

"OK, you know her best."

Joel walked out of the breakroom and Ravyn poured about half of her coffee in the sink and refilled her cup. She'd talked to Joel so long her coffee had gone lukewarm.

She added sugar and a little cream and walked back to her office. She really needed to assign out stories for the April issue and begin thinking about May.

Chase poked his head in Ravyn's office shortly after she sat at her desk.

"Hey, I heard the good news, congrats!"

"Did Joel tell you?"

"Yeah. Have you guys set a date yet?"

"We're not there yet, Chase."

"Fall weddings in Atlanta are nice. My wife and I got married in late October."

"Yeah, my sister got married in Greenville last October. I was her maid of honor. It was a lovely wedding and the weather was perfect."

"Oh yeah, I remember when you were gone then. Well, bring your fiancé — Marc is it? — around the office some time. I'd love to meet him. Maybe go for a beer or something."

"That's a great idea. We could all go out for pizza and beer and I could introduce him."

"Set it up. I'll be there. Lots of us from the office would come."

"OK, Chase. I'll get it on the calendar. Thanks for suggesting it."

"And congratulations again," Chase said, as he headed down the hall.

Ravyn smiled. She really enjoyed working with Chase, and by and large she liked her other co-workers. The one she hadn't gotten along with as much was Jennifer Bagley, but she was now in Dallas. Should she call her and tell her the engagement news? She didn't want to rub it in her face, especially since Jennifer and Joel had been an item and now, apparently, were not.

But if Joel had told Chase about her engagement, Ravyn imagined it was now making the office rounds and Jennifer would hear about it eventually. Would Jennifer be slighted that she'd heard the news before Ravyn told her?

Ravyn sighed. This was office politics that she didn't like to play. She picked up her phone and dialed the interoffice code for Jennifer.

Jennifer picked up right away, which surprised Ravyn, since Dallas was on Central time. That would mean Jennifer was getting into the office much earlier than when she worked in the Atlanta office.

"What's up?" Jennifer asked.

"I just wanted to tell you my good news. Marc and I got engaged last night."

"That's nice. I'm happy for you."

Ravyn was a bit taken aback by Jennifer's response. It was like Ravyn had just told her water was wet. No enthusiasm.

"Well, I just wanted you to know. Talk to you soon," Ravyn said, ready to end the conversation and regretting she'd called at all.

'No, no," Jennifer said. "Tell me more. I want to hear all about it."

Ravyn wasn't sure Jennifer really did want to hear all about it, so she went with the short version. "Well, he took me out to dinner for Valentine's Day at Atlanta Fish Market and he proposed over dessert."

"That sounds romantic."

"It was. The Atlanta Fish Market had these incredible chocolate-covered strawberries as a special dessert. They went great with the champagne that arrived at the table."

"That sounds way better than my Valentine's Day," Jennifer lamented.

Ravyn was silent for a moment, then decided she should ask about Joel. "Didn't Joel do something nice for you?"

"Joel. Well, he sent some flowers and wanted to come to Dallas, but you know," Jennifer trailed off.

"No, I don't know. I think he still really cares for you. He thinks you are seeing someone else. Are you?" Ravyn couldn't believe she was being so bold with her boss. Normally she would never ask such personal questions, but she felt she owed it to Joel as well.

"No, I'm not seeing anyone. Not really."

That didn't sound good. Very vague. Maybe Joel was right, Ravyn thought. Maybe Jennifer was seeing someone.

"I think you should talk to him. He says you haven't talked in a while. Jennifer, if you're going to break up with him, make it quick."

"Why? So, he can start dating someone else? Is *he* seeing someone?"

"No and no. I certainly didn't mean it like that. I think he's confused as to why he hasn't heard from you. And I think he does care for you. But if you don't have the same feelings, let him go. I think he's the kind of guy who defines himself with a woman in his life. He just doesn't know how to be alone. Do you know what I mean?"

"I think I do. And I'm not sure I can be that woman for him."

"Oh."

"Don't judge me, Ravyn."

"I'm not judging you."

"It feels like you are. I can't be the one who concedes in this relationship. I already did that in my last relationship. I need more from him and he's not willing to give that."

"Then I'm sorry for you both. I think he really misses you and, yes, I think in his way he loves you."

"Love? What do you know about love?"

Ravyn was insulted by Jennifer's comment. After all, Ravyn had called her to tell Jennifer she was engaged.

"I may not know all the ins and outs of love, but I do know I love Marc and he loves me."

"I wish you well. You'll need it."

And with that, Jennifer hung up the phone.

Ravyn sat in stunned silence at her desk. Had she just had that conversation with her boss? What a bitch, Ravyn thought. Ravyn remembered exactly why she and Jennifer hadn't gotten along.

And what was her problem? She had no idea what Jennifer's backstory was, but it didn't even remotely sound like it was a happy ending.

She's just a bitter middle-aged woman, Ravyn thought. God, I hope I never turn into her.

Ravyn met Julie at Seven Lamps restaurant in Buckhead in late February to celebrate her engagement. It was a communal table-style restaurant with high ceilings. It was almost always noisy. But Ravyn was enjoying the buffalo chicken sandwich and waffle fries, so Seven Lamps was quickly becoming a favorite since their favorite restaurant, Twist, had closed permanently.

"I want to ask you something," Ravyn said.

"Sure, what is it?"

"I've asked my sister Jane to be my matron of honor, but I'd also like you to stand up for me. And I'd like Ashley and Lexie to be flower girls."

Julie's eyes began to water. "Oh, Ravyn, I'd love to stand up for you. And I'm sure the girls would be thrilled to be part of the wedding. Have you and Marc picked a date? Will you be married in Atlanta or in South Carolina?"

"We don't have a date yet. And I'm pretty sure we're going to get married here in Atlanta. His parents are here, we're both here. Although I grew up in South Carolina I don't see myself getting married there. It made sense for Jane because she's still living there. My life is here now."

Julie and Ravyn were about halfway through their lunch when Julie suddenly doubled over, clutching her abdomen.

"What's wrong?" Ravyn asked with alarm. She was distressed to see her friend in sudden pain.

Julie panted out a reply. "Oh, God, I've been getting these for a couple of weeks. I'm supposed to see my doctor in two weeks. God, I can hardly breathe."

"Julie, should I call an ambulance?"

"Oh, God, no," Julie said, putting up her hand like a traffic cop. "It will pass. Give me a minute."

"Is it on your right side? Is it your appendix?"

"No," Julie tried to breathe through the pain. "It's on the left."

Ravyn spent an uncomfortable 10 minutes, while Julie breathed slowly and clutched her midsection. Julie didn't even touch the rest of her lunch.

The waiter finally came over and asked if Julie would like a box for her meal. Julie just shook her head.

Ravyn was alarmed. She paid the bill then offered to drive Julie home. She wasn't sure her friend was well enough to drive.

"Please let me drive you home," Ravyn said.

"No, I'm OK. And I'm mad at you for paying for your own engagement lunch."

"Julie, I'm worried about you."

"I'm fine. Really, I am. And I'm seeing the doctor soon. She'll know what to do."

"Is this your regular doctor or your OB/GYN?"

"My regular doctor."

"Can't you get in sooner? Like today? You're in pain."

"I had an appointment scheduled for a week ago, but I had to reschedule. Ashley was sick."

Ashley and Lexie were Julie's tween daughters. Ravyn remembered when Ashley had gotten strep throat.

Ravyn and Julie hugged in the parking lot, Ravyn careful not to squeeze too tight, since Julie still looked like she might be in pain.

"Text me when you get home," Ravyn said. "I want to be sure you got home safely. And I want to know what the doctor says."

"I'll text you," Julie said. "And thank you for wanting me to be a part of your big day. I'm honored."

"Of course I want you on my big day, but you take care, Julie, and let me know what's going on."

Ravyn and most of the *Cleopatra* staff met at Max's Coal Oven Pizzeria in downtown Atlanta. The pizzeria wasn't far from the office but most of them carpooled over since parking was tight.

They had planned to get together earlier, but finally settled on March 4. It was Friday and the pizza place was packed.

Several of her co-workers had gotten there around 4 p.m. and gotten several tables and put them together. Joel was there with most of his advertising staff.

They were mostly young blond women. Ravyn wasn't really surprised that Joel surrounded himself with young, beautiful women. Still, those young, beautiful women got their jobs done.

As her co-workers crowded around the pushed-together tables, it got noisier in the restaurant. They ordered several pizzas and pitchers of beer.

Kerry, one of the ad accountants, gushed at Ravyn's engagement ring.

"It's just beautiful. How many carats is it?"

"You know, I'm not sure. I know Marc has the paperwork because he needed to get it insured. I honestly never thought to ask because I love it no matter how many carats it has."

"It's just beautiful."

Ravyn had hoped Marc would make it tonight to meet her co-workers, but he was working late on a proposal for a new client. Then he planned to go to the gym. He was really into his new boxing class. She knew he wouldn't want to miss it. There'd be other times to meet her co-workers. And she kind of liked being the center of attention tonight.

Ravyn enjoyed a couple of glasses of beer and two slices of pepperoni pizza that night. She looked over the friends around the table, her eyes landing on Joel.

Joel looked at ease, flirting with the sales associates. Was anyone on the ad staff older than 30? She didn't think so.

Some of the women were single, Ravyn knew, but others were married with very young children. Kristine was pregnant with her second child and she wasn't yet 30. Or was she?

Kristine had a salad that night. "Pizza gives me heartburn while I'm pregnant," Kristine explained. Ravyn nodded, not that she'd know.

Ravyn wondered if Joel and Jennifer were over and if Joel was trying to move on. She knew he wouldn't be so stupid as to date anyone from the office again.

That was how he and Jennifer ended up in separate cities. Horizon Publications, the parent company, had a strict no relationship rule among its staff. Joel and Jennifer had flouted that rule and paid the price.

"Oh, don't worry about that," Joel said, placing his hand on Kerry's shoulder. "I know that client has been difficult. But I'd like to have his business. If you need me to come with you to the appointment, just say the word. Maybe we can do a good cop, bad cop kind of thing."

Kerry giggled in a high-pitched little girl laugh, flipping her blond hair back behind her ear. "Maybe we should both be bad cops and rough him up a little. That might be the only way."

"Kerry, we can't do that. I'm not going to bring a stick to beat him," Joel said.

Kerry turned to him, a frown forming between her eyebrows. "That guy is loaded and he doesn't want to spend a dime on advertising." She put her hands on her hips. "I keep showing him how he needs to spend money on advertising to get more exposure. I can't understand why he doesn't understand that."

"See if you can set up an appointment with him next Monday and I'll go with you," Joel said. "Maybe between your beauty and my brains, we'll close the deal."

Kerry giggled her childlike giggle again, but Ravyn just rolled her eyes. Joel had better be careful, she thought.

Chapter 5

Ravyn arrived home in mid-March and was surprised that Marc's BMW wasn't in the driveway. Ravyn walked into the house and contemplated dinner. She was tired. It had been a long day. She had forgotten to bring lunch that day and hadn't had time to run out for anything to eat. Right now, she was thinking of ordering a pizza and wings.

Ravyn walked back to the master bedroom and unhooked her bra. Slipping it off, she changed into her sweatpants and her favorite Peachtree Road Race T-shirt.

As she walked back to the kitchen, she heard Marc's car pull up.

"Hey, you're home late," Ravyn said.

"Sorry, I was really enjoying the boxing class. I got to spar with the instructor again after the class ended. He invited me to his boxing ring next week. He wants to spar with me and show me some more moves."

"Wow. You are really liking that class."

"I never thought boxing would be for me. I was always a weights and treadmill guy. But my instructor Jeff really gives us a workout. The footwork, the jabs, the punches. Feel that muscle," Marc said, flexing his arm at Ravyn. "Just feel that."

Ravyn felt his bicep, but it felt just as firm as it ever had when she'd held onto his arm. Of course, that was nearly always during sex, when her mind was not on how firm his arm was.

"Yes, that does feel firm," she said.

"Firm? It's rock hard. My arms have never been like this. I'm stronger and feel great."

"Well since you had a great workout, how about a pizza and wings tonight?"

"Babe, I need some lean protein. Jeff says I need to start eating clean and drop a few pounds," Marc said, patting his small belly. "I need to lose this."

Ravyn sighed. She really wanted to order out tonight. "Are you cooking?"

"Sure, I'll cook. I need to get cleaned up first. Will you get started with dinner, though?"

"Sure. I'll get the salad ready. You want chicken tonight? Or maybe some pork chops?"

"Pork chops, I think. Are they in the freezer?"

"I think so. Might have to defrost them in the microwave first."

"OK, can you do that? Maybe get some sweet potatoes out?"

Ravyn realized she was going to end up fixing the whole meal tonight. "Sure, I'll get dinner started. Go jump in the shower."

Ravyn got the pork chops out of the freezer and immediately put them in the microwave to defrost. She turned on the oven for the sweet potatoes and got a bag of frozen cauliflower out to put in the microwave for later.

When the pork chops were defrosted, she debated frying them, then decided to bake them in the oven. But she thought she should zap the sweet potatoes first in the microwave or they'd take forever in the oven. About 4 minutes later she popped them into the oven with the pork chops.

Ravyn realized she was really hungry when she began making dinner. She looked around for a small snack to eat to tide her over until she and Marc ate dinner. She grabbed a handful of walnuts out of the pantry. She eyed the pecans, thinking they might be good on the pork chops, especially if she put some peach jam on the pork chops and then the nuts.

Marc appeared about 20 minutes later with damp hair and smelling of his woodsy shower gel.

"Sorry I took so long. My muscles just needed the hot water to get the soreness worked out."

"It's OK. Dinner is in the works."

"Smells good."

"Pork chops, sweet potatoes, cauliflower and I'll make a small salad too."

Marc pulled Ravyn close in the kitchen. "You are incredible."

She smiled up at him. "I like to think so."

"How much longer until dinner?"

"Don't even think about it, Marc."

"You might be incredible, but you are a party pooper," he whispered. "Especially when I've got a hard on for you."

Ravyn looked down. Marc wasn't lying. He did have a very noticeable erection.

"I might have a few minutes to help you out there," she said.

Marc raised an eyebrow. "Really?"

"I'm setting the oven timer. I can give you about 15 to 20 minutes."

"I can work with that."

Ravyn could hear the oven timer as she laid in Marc's arms. It had been quick and hurried sex, but not unsatisfying. "I've got to get up," she told him, "or dinner will burn."

"Hmm. I don't want to get out of bed."

"Hey, I didn't have lunch today and now I really am hungry, so I'm getting up for dinner."

Marc rolled over and swung his legs over the bed, rolling up to sitting. He grabbed his own sweatpants and a T-shirt with the arms cut out, pulling it over his head.

Ravyn pulled on her discarded sweatpants and race T-shirt again and padded out to the kitchen, getting the food on the table. Marc came out seconds later. They had dinner on the small breakfast table. They hardly ever used the formal dining room table in the other room. Ravyn wondered if they ever would host dinners for their families or friends.

"I think we should invite Julie, Rob and their girls over for dinner soon," Ravyn said.

"What?"

"I think we should start inviting people over for dinner. You know, be sociable," she said.

"OK. I like Julie. I haven't met her husband. Or her kids."

"Why don't we have your boss, Kyle over for dinner, too. He's married, isn't he?

"He is. Her name is Amy."

"Kyle and Amy. Well, invite them over."

"I need to see when they are in town, or when he's in town. He's got some other investments and he travels a lot. He has a private plane, you know. Has a couple of pilots that fly him all over."

"Is Amy in Atlanta?" Ravyn asked.

"No. She's not, so we'll have to plan it and coordinate. Kyle will fly in with her. Might have to put them up at our house, maybe even the pilots."

"It might be a squeeze, but we've got two guest rooms. And it might be fun to have everyone here. We could do it."

"If you are sure. That's a lot of work to host people. Would you want to do it over a weekend?"

"We'd almost have to," she replied. "Let's see if they are free in April. That will give us about a month to get ready. We can host Julie and Rob and their kids later this month. It could kind of be a trial run for your boss and his wife."

"Let's do it."

Ravyn called Julie to see if she and her family were free for dinner April 2. She also wanted to ask what Julie had learned from her doctor.

"Oh, they just told me I was having a bad period," Julie said. "They said it was probably cramping. I'm not sure that's it. I've had cramps. This didn't feel like cramps. Although maybe it was. But it was just on my left side. I've never had cramps on just one side."

"Are you getting a second opinion?"

"My doctor gave me a prescription for the cramps. You know, I'll give it a try. I hope it's just that. If it's not that, they want to do an ultrasound."

"I think you should get a second opinion. You know your own body, Julie."

"Let's see if the prescription helps. If it doesn't, I'll do the ultrasound and if I need to then I'll get a second opinion. And we'd love to join you and Marc for dinner. That sounds like fun. Are you sure you want us to bring the girls? We could get a sitter."

"No, bring the girls. I'll stop at Michael's Craft store and get some puzzles or crafts for them. And we have a second bedroom if they get tired. Then we can just chat and have a nice evening."

"If it's not too much. Really, the girls can be a bit much."

"Seriously, we have this big dining room table that probably hasn't been used since Marc's divorce. I don't know that he and Karen ever used it for entertaining. It feels like a statement piece if you want my opinion. I want to use it to entertain. We can get everyone around it. I think me and Marc just need to have more couple friends. You'll be our first guests in this house."

"We can certainly be your couple friends. And we'd love to be your first guests, especially if you cook for us."

"You know I will cook for you. I think I'll do a pork roast or a pork tenderloin. Any objections?"

"Not at all. I look forward to it. Let me know, so I can bring wine."

"You don't have to bring wine. We began a wine club thing at the first of the year. We have plenty."

"No, no. I can't come empty handed."

"Oh, Julie, you are just like me. We've both lived in the South too long to come to dinner empty handed. I'll do pork, whether a roast or a tenderloin, so count on that."

Marc came home from work excited. His boss, Kyle Quitman, wanted him to go to Star 1 winery in Napa, California, where Black Kat Investors had just made an investment.

"He wants me to go out and look at the books, see if it's being run correctly. We'll be out there about a week," he said.

"We?"

"He said I can bring you. What do you say? Can you get off? It would be a great vacation and entirely paid for. He even said we could fly out on his private jet."

"When is this?"

"Mid-May."

"Let me go in tomorrow to find out, but I think I can. Do you have the dates?"

"That's being worked out. But I'll let you know soon."

"It sounds like a great trip. Will they put us up at a hotel?"

"They've got a B&B near the winery, so we'll stay there. I'll find the website so you can see it."

"A B&B sounds even better, very romantic. Are Kyle and Amy still planning to come to dinner in late April? Rob and Julie are coming April 2."

"Yeah, they've confirmed for April 30. I don't think they have any food allergies but I'll double check with Kyle."

"Great. I need to think about the menu. I want to make a good impression."

"I do, too. I need to find out what drinks they might want. I guess they are probably wine drinkers since Kyle's bought the majority interest in Star 1. That's the name of the winery. I know Kyle likes beer, too. We've gone out for beer a couple of times."

"You have?"

"Well, it was before you moved in. It was when we were negotiating for the company. We haven't gone out for beer since I sold the company."

"That's kind of too bad."

"Nah, it's OK. He's moved on to other companies, like this winery he's purchased."

"Winery? Is that a weird thing for an investor to buy?"

"It could be he's doing it for a tax write off. If it loses money, he could take it as a business write off."

"But you just said he's sending you out to look at the books and see how it's run. Doesn't sound like he wants it to lose money."

"No. I'm sure he doesn't."

"So, I've met him, but what is his wife like?"

"I've never met her."

"Oh, boy. I hope dinner goes OK."

"Listen, I'm more worried about dinner with Julie and Rob. He's not exactly a fan of mine, remember? I'm the one who sent roses to his wife and made him mad. I'm going to be lucky if he doesn't punch me."

Ravyn laughed at the memory. As Marc was wooing Ravyn last year with a fake Tinder profile, Julie had given Marc encouragement and advice. In fact, she encouraged him to create the fake profile using his brother Bruce's photos.

To thank Julie for her help, Marc had sent roses to her Buckhead house. Julie's husband Rob had seen the flowers and gotten jealous.

Julie had explained the flowers were a thank you for helping Marc. In the end, Rob had begun to be more attentive to his own wife, sending her flowers. They were even planning to take a long weekend in May to a resort in Mexico, with their daughters. The resort had kids' activities so Julie would get some free time, too.

"He won't punch you. Although Julie may kiss you for making him jealous and that might make him mad. That might make me mad, as well," Ravyn said, smiling up at him.

"I wouldn't want to make you jealous," Marc said, putting his hand up as if to fend off Julie. "I will avert any attention Julie might give me."

Ravyn rolled her eyes. "You idiot," she said, pushing his hand away. "I know Rob and Julie are in a good place. She said they're even going on a trip to Mexico next month, as a family."

"With the kids? Will that even be a vacation?"

"Julie seems to think so. The kids will have activities they can do."

"Well, good for them. And we'll have our trip to Napa."

Chapter 6

Ravyn was nervous all day Saturday, cleaning the house and checking the food she was preparing for Rob and Julie's dinner that night. She'd also gotten some puzzles and crafts at the Michael's store in Buckhead that morning.

In reality, she wasn't sure she wouldn't be asleep by the time her company arrived. She was running on empty since she hadn't slept well the night before. She was anxious about the dinner.

Ravyn really felt like Julie's family was her company. The dinner for Kyle and Amy Quitman later in April would be Marc's company. She felt like she'd just be the "hired help" at that dinner. Marc would do most of the work. For Rob and Julie's dinner, she would be the chef and hostess.

Marc and Ravyn's guests arrived around 6 p.m. Julie and Rob's girls Ashley and Lexie threw off their jackets and, spotting Felix, chased him into the guest bedroom.

Rob and Julie entered with two bottles of white wine. Marc and Rob shook hands, then clapped each other on the back, joking about the roses incident.

Ravyn showed Julie around the house and the adults ended up in the kitchen, opening a bottle of the white wine. Lexie ran in shortly after, crying that Felix had scratched her.

"Well, honey, you can't chase him and make him angry," Julie said.

Ravyn went to the bathroom and got a bandage. "I'm sorry sweetie," she said, placing the bandage on the top of her hand. "Why don't you leave Felix alone for a little while. I've got some puzzles and crafts for you and Ashley."

She led Lexie into the home office and pulled out a bag from Michael's. "Look, here is a jewelry making kit. Maybe you can make me and your mom some bracelets."

"Ashley, come see! We can make bracelets!" Lexie shouted to her sister.

Ravyn returned to the kitchen and nodded to Julie. "She's fine and now they are making us some bracelets.

"Auntie Ravyn to the rescue. Good call on the crafts. Although you and I may end up with a lot of bracelets tonight."

"I'll wear them with pride to work on Monday," Ravyn laughed.

They gathered around the table at 7:30 p.m. Ravyn had roasted two pork tenderloins with carrots and potatoes. She'd also made homemade tiramisu, an Italian dessert she'd learned to make at her cooking school over a year ago.

When they were finished with dessert, Ashley and Lexie ran off to do a puzzle before their bedtime. The adults sat around the table drinking the last of their wine and chatting.

Suddenly, Julie clutched at her abdomen, doubling over.

"Julie!" Ravyn cried out, alarmed.

Julie began panting, trying to breathe through the pain.

"Is this the problem she was having before?" Ravyn asked Rob.

Rob seemed alarmed as well. "I'm not sure. Julie, what can I do?"

Ravyn could see Rob's concern. She wasn't sure he knew what was happening either.

"Should I call an ambulance?" Marc asked.

"No, no," Julie said, trying to catch her breath. "I just need a minute." She held up her hand. "I'm OK. I'm OK."

Julie sounded like she was trying to convince herself.

"I'm not sure you are," Ravyn said.

"Get the girls, Rob. It's time to go home," Julie said.

Rob went to the home office and gathered their daughters. He got their jackets on, as Ravyn helped her friend into her coat.

"What can I do?" Ravyn asked.

"Nothing. I'll call the doctor tomorrow. I'm not getting better with the medicine."

"Have you talked to your OB/GYN?"

"No. Not yet."

"Please consider a second opinion."

"I will. Thank you for dinner tonight. Really, we had a great time," Julie said.

"Yes, thank you," Rob said, shepherding the girls out to the car.

Marc and Ravyn waved to their friends as they drove away. As soon as the car was out of sight, Ravyn began to cry.

"I'm so worried about her," she croaked.

Marc hugged her and rubbed her back. "It will be OK, babe. It will be OK."

Ravyn called Julie early Sunday to see how she was doing.

"I'm fine. I'm sorry I ruined dinner."

"You did not ruin dinner. We were finished. Did you call your doctor?"

"I'll have to call into my OB/GYN Monday. I hope she can get me in."

"I hope so, too."

"When are you having dinner with Marc's new boss?"

"In two weeks. I need to figure out the menu. Your family was easy. Since I don't really know them, I'm not sure what to fix."

"You could always do that roasted chicken recipe you got in Italy. That's really good."

"I could, but maybe they'll want something fancier. I'm not doing beef Wellington, or anything like that, but I may have to find a recipe online that isn't too complicated."

"You could order from a restaurant and pass it off as yours."

"That may be my last resort, especially if I burn anything."

"You won't burn anything. You're a better cook than you give yourself credit for. I'd be buying frozen lasagna and tossing a salad."

"That might not be a bad idea, the lasagna, I mean. I could make that ahead and then just pop it in the oven. A tossed salad would be great, too, and I'd just have to buy some Italian bread. Thanks for the idea."

"I'm here to help."

"Well, let me know what the doctor says. I was worried about you last night."

"I didn't mean to alarm you. It just comes on kind of suddenly when I move a certain way."

"And it's just on your left side?"

"It is."

"Do you think it's a cyst or something?"

"I've consulted with Dr. Google about that, but I don't think I have all the right symptoms."

"Well, your real doctor should be able to help. I hope."

"Yeah, I'll let you know what she says."

Julie called that Friday to let Ravyn know the doctor found an ovarian cyst on her left ovary. She'd found it with an ultrasound. Since cysts sometimes went away on their own, her doctor suggested waiting to see if it resolved on its own.

"And what if it doesn't go away on its own?" Ravyn asked.

Julie's voice got quiet. "I'd have surgery to remove the left ovary. I hope it doesn't come to that. Rob and I are finished having children but I don't want that taken away from me."

"Of course not, Julie," Ravyn said. "I hope that doesn't happen. It will be alright. It will go away. "

"I pray you are right."

Ravyn had nervous energy for the next two weeks contemplating the dinner menu for Kyle and Amy Quitman. Just when she thought she had it figured out, she waffled and changed her mind.

"Why are you driving yourself crazy about this?" Marc asked.

"I want to make a good impression. He's your boss! Don't you care what we fix?"

"Well, I certainly don't want you to fix mud pies. Just fix something normal."

"Normal? Normal? Jesus Christ, Marc, I can't fix something normal. I have to fix something that will impress them."

Marc rolled his eyes. He couldn't understand Ravyn's anxiety about this dinner. "Why don't you make something from your cooking school in Italy? What about that rice dish you made?"

"You mean, the risotto? Which one? The mushroom one, the asparagus one or the eggplant one? I've made you all three."

Marc looked at her blankly. "They were different?"

"Oh my God, Marc! Why do I even try? Why?"

"OK, I'm sorry. I didn't realize they were different. They were all good. I'm sure they were good. I'll pay attention next time. You know, I never even had risotto before we started living together."

"That's not making me feel any better."

"OK, what about rice, I mean risotto, as a side dish and some grilled chicken. I could do that on the grill. Maybe the mushroom one. That would be great with the chicken. And then a side vegetable. Maybe steamed broccoli."

Ravyn looked at Marc, then burst into tears.

"What's the matter?"

"You figured out a better menu than I did."

Marc pulled Ravyn into him. "Is it that time of the month? You are awfully weepy."

Ravyn stopped crying and wiped her eyes on Marc's sweater. "Sorry. I guess I have been weepy lately. God, I hate the pill. It makes me all crabby and then weepy."

"I'm sorry you are having a bad time. Should you see your doctor again? Maybe she can recommend some other pill."

"I'm on the lowest dose possible."

"But is there another brand or something?"

"I'll call my doctor tomorrow. Maybe there is something that will make me less crazy."

"You are not crazy. I just don't like seeing you so upset."

"Well, I think you've come up with our menu, so thank you."

"I'm glad that's done. I think they'll like it."

"Have you even talked to them?"

"I've talked to Kyle. He and his wife will be here April 30."

"Will they need to stay at our place?"

"No. They'll stay at the Mandarin Oriental, along with their pilots."

"Ooh, fancy," Ravyn said. She was referring to the very upscale hotel in Buckhead not far from their house in Garden Hills. "And the pilots will stay there too?"

"Yeah, I guess Kyle and Amy like to stay there when they are in town."

"They don't have an apartment here in Atlanta?"

"Nope. They live in Austin, Texas, and just stay at nice hotels when they travel."

"Must be nice," Ravyn said, dryly.

"Well, we'll be staying at a nice B&B next month. Did you ask for the time off?"

"Yes, and I got it. So, we're good to go."

Marc pulled Ravyn into him again. "I'm glad. I want us to have a little time to ourselves. After all, we just got engaged."

"Like a mini honeymoon?"

"Like a mini honeymoon. Should we practice now?"

"The honeymoon? We could." Ravyn smiled and took Marc by the hand and led him into the master bedroom.

Kyle and Amy Quitman showed up at Marc and Ravyn's door right on time.

Kyle was dressed in dark jeans and a periwinkle blue sweater. It complemented his blue eyes. He also had light brown short cropped hair. Ravyn thought maybe he'd gotten it cut that day.

Amy had long wavy brown hair. She wore a navy midi dress with mid-calf boots. She looked so stylish, Ravyn began to feel dowdy next to her.

Ravyn wore the teal sweater Marc had given her a couple of Christmases ago and black pants. She wore black shoe boots, too.

Marc had on his standard beige khaki pants and muted green sweater. It really brought out the gold in his hazel eyes. A pair of brown loafers rounded out his outfit.

At first, the conversation between the couples was a bit awkward. They talked about Atlanta's traffic, the weather in Texas and the winery Kyle had recently invested in.

"We brought some bottles from Star 1," Amy said, holding up a canvas bag with the Star1 logo on the front. "Reds and whites. I hope that is OK."

"That sounds great," Ravyn said. "We're excited to visit the winery next month. I've never been to California."

"Oh, you'll love it," Amy said. "Star 1 is beautiful."

"Have you been there, too?" Ravyn asked.

"Kyle's been there a few times, but I went with him right before he made the investment. Then we stayed there shortly after," Amy answered. "It's beautiful. Are you staying at the B&B?"

"We are," Marc said. "Looking forward to it. Sort of a mini pre-honeymoon since we just got engaged."

"Oh! Show me the ring!" Amy exclaimed.

Ravyn held her hand over the table. Amy grabbed Ravyn's left hand and oohed and ahhed over it. "It's gorgeous. Kyle, clearly you are paying Marc too much."

Kyle just smiled.

Marc smiled stiffly. "Well, I'm just glad Ravyn likes it. I surprised her with the ring. I wasn't sure she'd like it."

"I love it. Could not have asked for a better ring."

"It is beautiful. You are a lucky woman, Ravyn," Amy said.

The two couples enjoyed their evening. Amy and Kyle raved over the mushroom risotto and Ravyn recounted her cooking school in Italy, the recipes she'd learned and the cookbooks she'd purchased from her instructor.

Ravyn did not tell them about her Italian lover Luca she'd met during that trip. Luca had been an undercover cop investigating a couple of international jewel thieves at the cooking school.

Ravyn had been hurt that she'd been used and betrayed by Luca. She'd had feelings for him. She'd never even told Marc about Luca.

But she and Amy talked about the recipes she learned and how much they both loved Rome. "I would go back in a heartbeat," Ravyn said. "Hey, maybe Marc and I should go to Rome for our honeymoon."

Marc looked up. "Rome?"

"Oh my God! That would be so great! I could show you the city. We could go to St. Peter's Basilica. Oh, maybe we could take the train up to Florence. That would be fun," Ravyn said, her voice getting excited and high pitched.

"We can talk about it later," Marc said. "I know you love it there."

"And I've never been to Florence," Ravyn said. "Maybe we can even go on up to Venice."

"Ugh," Amy said. "Don't go in the summer. The Venice canals stink in the summer."

"We haven't picked a date for the wedding yet," Ravyn said.

"Go in the fall," Amy said. "The canals won't smell and there won't be as many tourists. Really, that's the same advice for all of Italy."

"Yeah. I went to Rome in November of 2014 and it was great," Ravyn said. "There were tourists, but it wasn't crowded. We got into all the attractions pretty quickly."

"We?" Marc asked, puzzled.

Ravyn hesitated, trying to recover from her faux pas. She'd gone everywhere in Rome with Luca. "I went with some of my classmates from the cooking school."

"Of course," Marc said.

Amy and Ravyn stood in the kitchen chatting after dinner and Ravyn loaded the dishwasher. Marc and Kyle remained in the living room, finishing the next to last bottle of wine.

With the last bottle of wine, Marc suggested they move out to the deck and light the fire pit. The air was crisp and perfect for a fire.

Marc and Kyle got the fire pit going while Amy and Ravyn got comfortable in the outdoor chairs. There was a slight chill in the late April air and Ravyn handed Amy a lap blanket.

"I hope you don't mind that you'll be working while you are at Star 1," Kyle said, as Marc poked the fire logs. "I know the books are all in order, but I'd like you to observe the winery's operations, make sure the place is being run efficiently."

"I'm happy to do that. Do you want me to report back daily?"

"No, no. We'll talk when you get back. I think the owner, Robert Pierce, can suggest some side trips for you and Ravyn."

"Aren't you the owner now?" Marc asked.

"Well, yes, but I don't know a thing about winemaking, so the owner, Bobby, well, he's the minority owner now, is still doing what he does. I just want to make sure it will all turn a profit."

"Guess I should do a little research on winemaking, because I don't know anything about it either. I know I enjoy drinking wine. That's about it."

"I don't think you need to do that. I just want to know about the operations and if they could be profitable in the next five years."

"Oh, you want the winery profitable in five years?"

"Sooner if possible," Kyle said.

"Are you two just going to talk business?" Ravyn asked. "Look up at the stars!"

"Sorry, no more business talk," Kyle said, opening the last bottle of wine. He poured the first two glasses and handed them to Amy and Ravyn.

"Thank you. Are you and Amy here all weekend?" Ravyn asked.

"No, we're going to head back to Texas tomorrow," Amy said.

"I'm glad you could take time out and come to dinner," Marc said. "I know Ravyn has wanted us to be more social. I think she just wants to keep up her cooking skills."

"Yes, the meal was terrific," Amy said. "This was really nice. We don't get out with other couples as much as I'd like, either."

The two couples could hear a siren in the distance, and it seemed to be getting closer.

Ravyn looked over and could see a fire truck pulling up at a home behind theirs. Then another fire truck pulled behind it.

"Wonder what's going on?" Marc said. "Looks like they've pulled up to the Caters' house."

"I hope Eleanor and Arthur are OK," Ravyn said.

They went back to their conversation when the flashing lights were suddenly in front of Marc and Ravyn's home. The couples turned to see three firefighters in full turnout gear, one carrying an ax, rounding the house and stopping when they saw Marc, Ravyn, Amy and Kyle sitting on the deck around the firepit.

"Is everything OK here?" one firefighter asked.

Marc and Ravyn looked at each other, then at the firefighters.

"We're fine," Marc said, standing up. "Is there a problem?"

"We got a call there was a fire," the firefighter said.

"We've just been out here with the firepit," Marc said. "We've had it a few nights this spring. We've never had anyone call about it before."

"Well, I guess your neighbors were concerned. Looks like the firepit is following the local ordinance. Sorry to have disturbed your evening."

The firefighters departed and soon the trucks did as well.

"That was odd," Ravyn said. "The Caters have never called the fire department on us before."

"Our homeowners association is very strict," Amy said. "We can't do a lot of things. Our yard crew can't mow or blow leaves before 10 a.m."

Ravyn almost made a comment about having a yard crew, but stopped herself, instead commenting on how good the wine tasted.

"This merlot is one of my favorites," Amy said.

After the wine was gone, the couples rose to return to the house. Ravyn came from the guest bedroom with Kyle and Amy's jackets.

"We're flying out early tomorrow," Amy said. "But thank you for a lovely evening."

Marc and Ravyn stood at their front door as Kyle and Amy waved from their Zipcar.

"That was fun. I like them," Ravyn said.

"Yeah. I enjoyed it too," he said, hugging her. "I hope we can do it again sometime. Did you save room for dessert?"

"Honey, we had dessert. The tiramisu, remember?"

"Are you sure? Don't you want a second dessert?"

"Maybe, if you rub my feet. These boots are pinching my toes."

Marc made Ravyn sit down on the couch, then he got down on one knee and unzipped her shoe boot. Then he unzipped the other. He rolled her left foot and began to massage it. Ravyn leaned back on the couch and nearly moaned with pleasure. Marc really did give good foot rubs. She smiled thinking about how good he was with his hands.

'What's that smile for?"

"It means you are hitting all the right spots on my foot. That feels really good."

"If you think I hit the right spots on your foot, I can show you how I can make you feel even better on other body parts."

"Do the right foot first and then I'll let you make me feel fantastic."

Marc reached for Ravyn's right foot and worked his thumbs into her heel and then the arch of her foot.

"Oh my God, that feels great. And I'm ready to feel fantastic now."

Marc took Ravyn's hand and pulled her up from the couch. They held hands as they entered the bedroom.

Chapter 7

Ravyn woke Sunday morning with Marc's arms wrapped around her. She felt his soft breath in her hair. She liked the way she could curl up perfectly with his legs. The perfect spoon.

Sunlight peeked through the curtains in the bedroom. She thought it was probably later than she expected.

They'd had that wine last night and then made love. By the time they had gotten to sleep it was very late.

That was what Sunday mornings were for, she thought. A soft awakening to a new day. They wouldn't have anything pressing to do today. Maybe they'd have brunch somewhere in Buckhead.

Ravyn untangled herself from Marc and lay on her back fully stretching out her arms and feet. Marc stirred beside her.

"Good morning, my love."

"Good morning to you, too," she said rolling toward his warm body.

"What are we doing today?" he asked.

"What do you want to do? Are you going to the gym?"

"Maybe later. Are you going for a run?"

"Maybe later," she said. "Sounds like we're being lazy and staying in bed."

"Well, not too lazy. I've got to mow the backyard before it gets too warm," Marc said.

"Why don't you hire a lawn service?" Ravyn asked. "Like Kyle and Amy do. I can't imagine a service would charge that much for your small yard."

"Well, it's the only time I can wear a wife beater shirt and let the neighbors see my big guns," Marc said, smiling, flexing his biceps like a bodybuilder.

"You are awful," Ravyn said, tossing her pillow at him.

"So, it's a fight you want, huh?" Marc asked, grabbing his pillow and hitting her with it.

"Ah!" she shouted, trying to grab back her pillow, but Marc now held both pillows and was windmilling Ravyn with them. Ravyn stumbled out of bed and ran for the bathroom, slamming the door.

"You can't hide in there forever," he said.

"Oh yes I can!" she shouted through the door.

"You're no fun. Come out for round two."

"I can tell you have been practicing your boxing. Those pillows are soft, but you hit me hard."

"I did?" Marc asked softly, looking down at the pillows he was holding in his hands. He dropped them to the floor.

"You did. I don't think enough for a bruise, but you did put your arms in it," Ravyn said, opening the door a crack. She waved a white washcloth at him. "I surrender."

"I'm sorry," he said, pushing the bathroom door open wider, then pulling her in for a bear hug. "Truce?"

"Truce," she said, smiling up at him.

Marc finished mowing the backyard then came in for a shower. Ravyn sniggered because she didn't see him out there in his white "wife beater" tank top. He wore his ratty University of Georgia T-shirt. The bulldog on the front was so faded she wished she could toss it and buy him a new one.

Ravyn had showered earlier and wore black capris and a running shirt.

"You want to do lunch here or go out?" Marc said, a white towel wrapped around his waist. He vigorously dried his hair with a smaller towel. Ravyn looked at Marc and for a moment forgot about eating altogether. But she was hungry.

"Oh, I'll always vote for brunch out on a Sunday. We can eat at home tonight. I'll take some hamburger out of the freezer. Unless you want the leftover chicken and risotto from last night?"

"You take that for lunch tomorrow. Let's have burgers. I need something different from last night. Did you get the lean burger meat?"

"I did," she said, as she reached into the freezer and took out a pound of hamburger meat, placing the package in the refrigerator. "When we get back from brunch, I'll patty them up and put some seasoning on them. I've got to thaw it out first."

They decided on brunch at Flying Biscuit Cafe in Midtown. Ravyn used to walk over to the restaurant from her condo, but now they had to find parking and walk over, then wait for a table for about 45 minutes.

They enjoyed the rest of their Sunday, Ravyn finishing the week's laundry while Marc got the burgers on the grill.

Monday afternoon, Ravyn got a call at her office from Julie.

"What's up?" Ravyn asked.

"I have some bad news," Julie began.

"Oh, God, what is it?" Ravyn asked, suddenly afraid for her friend.

"Remember that ovarian cyst I've got?"

"Yes. Is it worse?"

"Well, I finally went back to my OB/GYN for another ultrasound and she determined I have a very large ovarian cyst. It's not shrinking."

"Not shrinking? What does that mean?"

"Because it's so large, she's afraid it will rupture, so she's recommending I have it removed."

"Removed? As in surgically?"

"Yes. So, I have a huge favor to ask."

"Whatever it is I'll do it."

"I'm having surgery sooner rather than later, so my cyst doesn't rupture. And I'll need someone to watch the girls. I mean, stay at my house and make sure they get to school. Rob will take off work so he can be with me at the hospital, but I'll need help."

"Of course. Just give me the dates, I'll be there."

"I'm having surgery May 20 and I'll be in the hospital for at least two days, so I'd only need help May 20 and 21."

"Oh," Ravyn said.

"Can you do it?" Julie asked, worried that her friend might say no.

Ravyn hesitated. That was the weekend she and Marc were supposed to go to Napa. "OK, I'll be there. I can get off work. Let me just talk to Marc. He'll want to know, too."

"I can't thank you enough," Julie said, relieved. "I know the girls would be comfortable with you there. I haven't told them I'm having surgery yet. I didn't want to scare them."

"Well, you've sort of scared me."

"It will be OK," Julie said. She suddenly started crying.

"What's wrong? Are you in pain?"

"No. I'm just really sad, and scared, about this surgery."

"I thought you said it was going to be OK."

"It will be. But given my age and losing an ovary, I probably won't be able to have any more children, Ravyn," Julie sobbed.

"Oh no. I'm so sorry."

"I mean, Rob and I are finished with our family. We love our girls. But I didn't want this surgery to take away my options. I didn't want it to be the end. I'm not even 40!"

"I'm so sorry, Julie. I really am. Can I take you out to dinner tonight?"

"No, I'm not in the mood for dinner out. I'm kind of hiding in my room at night crying since I got the news."

"Do you want me to come over? I'll bring takeout and wine."

"That might be good. Can we do it on Friday? Then you won't have to work and we can drink and not worry about it. Plan to stay over."

"OK, I'll talk to Marc about it."

"Thank you so much. This puts my mind at ease."

Ravyn hung up with her best friend but felt sick that she would miss the trip with Marc. She had really been looking forward to it. But she couldn't let Julie down. And she was sure there would be other opportunities to visit the winery in Napa. Ravyn just had to get the courage to tell Marc she couldn't go.

"Ravyn, I can't believe you aren't going!" Marc shouted. "This was supposed to be a trip for the both of us."

"Marc, it's not like I don't want to go. Julie's having surgery. Surgery! Her husband will be with her and they can't leave their daughters alone."

"I'm not saying they should leave their daughters alone, but don't they have grandparents or someone else who could look after them?"

"Rob's parents live in an assisted living apartment in Nashville and Julie's parents are in Florida. And she asked me. I feel honored she'd entrust them to me. Look, won't there be other times we can go to Napa? Or can we go the following week?"

"I can't rearrange this trip. I'm supposed to be there May 20. I can't change the plans. Besides, the B&B is booked up for Memorial Day weekend. We were lucky to get this weekend. This was the weekend for us."

"I'm sorry, Marc. I'll have to miss the trip. I hate it. I want to go. I really do. I'm not happy about missing it. I wanted to go with you. Please don't be angry."

Marc was angry. He didn't want to go to California without Ravyn. He wanted to go as a couple. It wouldn't be nearly as fun without her and he'd be lonely on his own. He had to go, of course. Now he'd just have to concentrate on the work he needed to do while there. He sighed.

"I am angry with you. You just told Julie yes, didn't you? You didn't even ask me, Ravyn. You didn't talk to me first. We're getting married. We're supposed to be a team."

"I'm sorry I didn't talk to you first, but she's having surgery. And she's very upset about it because it will mean she probably won't be able to have any more children."

"You made a decision that affects me, though. Without consulting me."

Ravyn started to cry. "I'm sorry."

"It's like you put her friendship first, ahead of me, your future husband. Can you see why I'm angry?"

Ravyn just cried and nodded. She couldn't speak.

Marc went silent. "I guess there's nothing I can do to convince you to come with me. You chose Julie over me."

"I'm really sorry. I just can't let Julie down."

"Well you are letting me down," Marc said as he walked to his wet bar and poured a large scotch. He gulped it down, then poured another.

Ravyn went to bed early that evening, her head pounding from crying. Marc stayed up later, drinking. Ravyn, feigning sleep, heard him come into the bedroom, heard him rustle around, then leave.

What was he doing? She wondered. Then she heard the guest bedroom door open and close.

She began crying again, even harder into her pillow.

Marc tossed and turned in the guest bed. He wasn't used to not having Ravyn sleep next to him. But he was so angry he didn't want to be near her that night. Now he thought of the old advice never to go to bed angry with the one you love. He'd not only gone to bed angry; he'd gone to bed in another room.

Marc finally fell into a restless sleep and then heard the alarm on his iPhone alert him it was time to get up. He planned to go to the gym and his boxing class. He knew he'd likely take his frustration out on his partner.

He got up and grabbed his gym bag, the bag he'd fumbled with in the dark bedroom the night before. He quickly left the house. He didn't hear whether Ravyn was up or not. He'd see her when he got back from the gym. Maybe he'd be less angry after a good workout.

Marc worked out hard at the gym. His boxing partner complained about how hard Marc was punching the pads he held up. His partner finally dropped his arms. "Sorry, man. You are killing my hands and arms. What's got you so fired up this morning?"

"I had a big fight with my girlfriend. I mean, my fiancée. Just working out some frustration and anger," Marc replied. "Sorry. I'll tone it down."

"Sorry, man. You'll have to pick another partner. You're killing my shoulders. They hurt."

Marc decided to quit when he couldn't find another partner who would spar with him. The other guys in the gym had seen how much he'd put into his workout. And the two women who also took the class shook their heads at him, even when he said he'd take it easy.

Marc decided to shower at the gym rather than at the house. He was delaying the inevitable discussion with Ravyn. He knew he was going to have to apologize, but he honestly thought she was in the wrong.

She should have discussed it with him. He probably would have acquiesced. He understood it was Julie and how serious the surgery was. Ravyn should have discussed it with him, he thought.

Marc drove down Pine Tree Drive toward his Garden Hills home. As he began to pull into his driveway, he saw Ravyn's Honda was gone. "Goddammit," he said under his breath.

Ravyn had awoken from a bad dream, rolled over to a cold space in the bed. Then she sat up with a start before she remembered Marc hadn't slept in their bed last night.

She listened but didn't hear him stirring in the house. "Marc?" she called out timidly.

Ravyn pulled on her robe and stuck her head into the hall. "Marc?" The house was quiet. Ravyn realized he wasn't in the house. She padded into the kitchen but the coffeemaker was empty. Marc hadn't started coffee, as he usually did when he got up first.

Ravyn pulled down a coffee filter and started coffee. She only made half a pot since Marc wasn't here to drink it with her. She drank one cup, then put the rest in her travel coffee mug.

She took a shower and quickly got dressed in her running gear. She was out the door with her coffee well before she normally went to work, but if Marc didn't want to see her this morning, she didn't want to see him either.

Marc walked into the house and threw his gym bag on the bistro table. He could smell coffee, so he knew Ravyn couldn't have been gone long. He looked in the coffee pot and saw there was none left. She didn't even leave some for him.

Marc got dressed and went to his office at Colony Square in Atlanta's Midtown. He stopped at Starbucks on his way up to his office. He was still in a foul mood. He was ready to apologize to Ravyn that morning but finding her gone just made him angrier. Now he wasn't ready to apologize.

Is this how it's going to be, he wondered? We're going to have a fight and she's going to run away? He asked himself. He suddenly wanted to talk to Julie.

Julie knew Ravyn best of all. But he couldn't call or text her. Not when Julie had been the reason for the fight between Ravyn and Marc. Plus, Marc was fairly certain Ravyn would be calling Julie that morning and Julie would take Ravyn's side.

Since Ravyn had left the house in her running clothes, she decided to run in Piedmont Park first before she went to her office downtown. She found a parking spot off Park Drive in Midtown. The spot meant she didn't have to pay for a parking spot.

She locked her Honda and headed into the park, running around the outside of the park and then into the active oval. She got three miles in before she got back to her car. Ravyn was annoyed she no longer lived in Spire. She wanted a nice shower.

Instead, she was going to have to head to her office and use the small fitness center shower. Ravyn didn't really prepare for showering and then drying her hair and putting on makeup in the tiny bathroom and shower.

Ravyn was grateful she kept a small makeup bag at her desk. In her dating days, she counted on that bag to refresh her look before an evening out.

She got up to her office around 8 a.m., well before her normal time. Even with the run she was early. It was quiet in the office. Almost too quiet.

Ravyn went into the break room and got another cup of coffee. This was a morning when she would need it. When she got back to her office, she called Julie. She knew the mom of two young girls would be up by now.

"Hey, Ravyn, what's up?" Julie asked, answering her cell phone.

"I just needed to talk. Marc and I had a big fight last night."

"Oh no. Are you OK?"

"I'm not sure. He didn't come to bed last night. He slept in the guest bedroom. When I got up this morning he was already gone. I guess he went to the gym but I don't really know."

"He didn't come to bed?"

"No, he didn't."

"What was the fight about?"

Ravyn hesitated. The fight had been about Julie and Ravyn was reluctant to tell her friend that, even though Ravyn really needed to talk about it.

"OK, don't be upset, but it was about you."

"Me? Why was it about me?" Julie asked. Then she paused. "Was it about your staying with the girls for my surgery?"

"Yes. Marc and I are supposed to leave for our Napa trip that day."

"Ravyn! Why didn't you tell me? I can find someone else to stay with the girls. I don't want to come between you and Marc."

"Julie, I want to stay with the girls. I really thought Marc would understand, but he got mad."

"I can see why. Let me find someone else to watch the girls."

"No!" Ravyn shouted. "It's done. I'm not going on the trip. I want to be there for you and Marc just needs to understand."

Julie wrinkled her forehead, although Ravyn couldn't see that. "Please let me find some other way."

"No. I won't hear of it. I'll be there."

"Ravyn, you are so stubborn."

"I am. That's why you love me."

Julie snorted out a laugh. "Well, I do love you. But I don't want to come between you and Marc."

"You can't come between me and Marc. After all, you brought us together. And he'll just have to see how stubborn I can be."

"God help him."

Now it was Ravyn's turn to laugh.

"Have you talked to him this morning?" Julie asked.

"No, I called you first for moral support. He hasn't called or texted."

"You should probably call him."

"Why me? He should call me."

"Ravyn, you are being stubborn again. Call him. Talk to him. You both need to clear the air, especially if you didn't sleep in the same bed last night. You don't want this to become a bigger issue between you two."

"You're right. I know you're right. I just don't want to be the bigger man, or woman, as it were."

"Ravyn, let me tell you a secret about marriage. Men are big babies. You are always going to have to be the bigger woman. You are always going to have to forgive bad behavior."

"Are you speaking from experience?"

"You know I am. I had to forgive my husband for fucking another woman. If that isn't forgiving bad behavior, I don't know what is."

"OK. I'll call him after you."

"Love you, Ravyn. And if I can find someone else to watch the girls, I will."

"Nope. I already have the time off and I'm going to watch them. You said it yourself. They will be more comfortable with me there, especially if Rob is at the hospital with you."

Ravyn hung up with Julie but didn't call Marc right away. She still thought he should call her to apologize. An hour later, with no word from him, she picked up her phone to call him.

"Hello, Ravyn," Marc said.

"Good morning," she answered. "You were gone when I got up."

"I went to the gym. Needed to work out some frustration. You were gone when I got home."

"I went for a run in Piedmont Park. I had to work out some frustration, too."

"I'm sorry," they said at the same time.

"I'm sorry about last night," Ravyn said, interrupting Marc. "I should have talked to you before I committed to Julie."

"And I'm sorry I blew up at you. I know she's your best friend. I just wanted us to have this vacation together."

"I know. I wanted it, too. So, what do we do now?" Ravyn asked.

"Well, you will stay in Atlanta with Julie's kids and I'll go to Napa and stay all alone at the B&B drinking good wine."

"Are we good?" Ravyn asked, worried.

"We're good, Ravyn. Even though you made me really angry, I still love you."

"And I love you."

"We did miss one of the best parts of our fight, though," Marc said.

"What's that?"

"Make-up sex."

"Oooh, make-up sex. Is it too late?"

"I'll let you know tonight when we get home," Marc said. Ravyn could almost see him smiling through the phone.

Chapter 8

In the next week, Marc packed for his trip to Napa and Ravyn packed a large overnight bag to stay at Julie's house. She was going to stay in their guest bedroom, since she expected Rob would be at the hospital with Julie most of the days she was there.

He'd be tired when he got home, so Ravyn planned on fixing dinner for the whole family and taking care of the house until Julie returned. How hard could it be?

Ravyn even thought she might stay one extra day after Julie was released from the hospital. She couldn't imagine that Julie would bounce back and be able to run her household for a couple of days at least.

The morning of May 19, Ravyn asked if Marc needed a ride to the airport the next day.

"I'll take Uber. I can write it off as a business expense," he said. "Besides, I'm flying out of PDK on Kyle's private jet."

"Oh, you are taking the private jet," Ravyn said. "Now I wish I was going. I can still drop you off at PDK," she said, referring to Atlanta's public use airport known as DeKalb-Peachtree Airport. But the airport was commonly called Peachtree-DeKalb Airport, or PDK. "That will be easier than trying to get you to Hartsfield-Jackson. You never know how the traffic will be on 285."

"Won't you be at Julie's all day tomorrow?" he said.

"Actually, I'm going over tonight so I can take the girls to school in the morning. Once I drop them off, I can come get you and take you to PDK," she said. "Your flight's in the morning, right?"

"Yes. 10 a.m. Are you sure you can take me?"

"I'm sure. Rob and Julie have to be at Piedmont Hospital around 6 a.m. for surgery. I'll have to get the girls up for school, but once they are there I won't have to be back at their house until I get them at 2 p.m."

"Won't the school bus pick them up?"

"They attend Lovett," Ravyn said, referring to a private Atlanta school. "I have to drop them off and pick them up."

"Ah," Marc said.

"Can you pick me up on the 25th, too?" Marc asked. "I think the flight will land later in the afternoon."

"Sure. I'm sure I'll be home from Julie's by then. I think I'll stay with them until Sunday, probably. Unless they kick me out. Or Julie does. I'll have to run home to feed Felix a couple of times."

Ravyn kissed Marc goodbye May 19 and headed to Julie's house. She walked into the home and immediately felt nervous tension in the house.

"Is everything OK?" she asked her friend when they were alone.

"I'm just," Julie said, her lower lip quivering before she burst into tears. Julie held her face in her hands.

Ravyn went over and held her friend while she sobbed. She stroked Julie's back, holding her close. "What's wrong?"

"We went for pre-op today and the OB/GYN thinks we should take both ovaries out."

"Why?"

"I didn't realize it when they did the ultrasound, but there was something on the right ovary, too."

"They don't think it's cancer, do they?" Ravyn asked, alarmed.

"They will biopsy it, but they want to take both ovaries," Julie said. She began sobbing harder. "I honestly thought I was only going to lose one ovary. And I was hoping against all hope I could still have children if I wanted to. But that won't happen now."

Ravyn held Julie just a bit closer. "I'm so sorry. I'm just so sorry. This is so unfair."

"And I can tell Rob's upset, too, but he's trying not to show it."

"Was he hoping for more kids?"

"I think he always was hoping for a son, even though we agreed our family was complete. I just think he always wanted a son."

"Oh, Julie. I'm sorry for both of you. What can I do for you? Can I get you some wine?"

"Yes, I could really use a glass. My doctor gave me some Xanax so I can sleep tonight."

"Maybe wine isn't a good idea then."

"Oh no, I want some wine," Julie said emphatically.

"OK, I'll get a small glass then."

"You'd better bring the bottle. This isn't the night to do a small glass. If I'm losing my fertility, I'm going to get raging drunk."

Ravyn eyed her friend. She'd make sure that didn't happen. But she hated that Julie was hurting. "I'm here for you. I'll get the girls up tomorrow, fix them a good breakfast and get them to Lovett."

Julie began to sob again.

"What's the matter?"

"I made you miss your trip! I'm sorry I came between you and Marc."

"Julie, it's OK. We've made up. We even had make-up sex."

Julie smiled wanly. "Was it good?"

Ravyn smiled. Her friend was slowly returning to her sarcastic self.

"It was excellent."

"Did he go down on you?"

"Oh yes. Yes, he did. My needs were met. I may have to pick a fight with him again."

"Don't you do that!"

The next morning Julie and Rob were gone before daylight. Julie had kissed and hugged her daughters hard when they went to bed the night before, explaining Ravyn would be there to take them to school in the morning.

Ravyn had trouble sleeping that night. She was worried about Julie. She missed Marc's body next to hers. She worried she wouldn't hear her alarm to get Lexie and Ashley up for school in the morning. She fell into a fitful sleep shortly before her iPhone alarm went off.

Ravyn dragged herself out of bed, padding down into the kitchen to start coffee. The pot only had a small amount in it. She supposed Rob had made coffee for himself, since Julie couldn't eat or drink anything before surgery.

She dumped the dregs out of the coffee pot and started a fresh pot. The rich earthy coffee aroma filled her nostrils. She was going to need it strong this morning.

Ravyn woke the girls, whipped scrambled eggs and poured orange juice, then loaded the girls into her Honda for school. Thankfully, the girls were old enough they didn't need booster seats anymore, but she still made them ride in the backseat, despite their protesting.

Ravyn was kind of glad she'd put her foot down on that issue. She remembered how she and her sister Jane had always fought over riding shotgun in the passenger seat. With Lexie and Ashely in the back seats, she didn't have to referee who would ride in the passenger seat next to her.

When she got the girls safely to school, after waiting in the drop-off line longer than she expected, she drove back to Garden

Hills to pick up Marc. He'd already called her once asking where she was.

Ravyn realized she was going to cut it close to get him to PDK. She pulled into the driveway and Marc was waiting on the porch with his suitcase.

"I'm sorry I'm late," Ravyn said as Marc put his bag in her trunk. "I didn't realize the drop-off line for the girls would be so long. I thought I'd be in and out. Clearly I don't know anything about having young children at a private school."

"It's OK. Let's just go."

Ravyn got onto Interstate 85 and headed north, getting onto Clairmont Road, turning onto the frontage road eventually turning onto Airport Road and past the PDK gates. She pulled up to the small terminal for the private planes.

She popped her trunk as Marc got out to get his suitcase. She went around to meet him at the back of her car.

"I'll miss you," she said.

"I'll miss you more," Marc said. "I wish you were coming with me."

"I wish I was, too. I'm sorry this got so messed up."

"Take care of Julie and her kids and I'll see you next week."

"Call or text me when you land. I'll worry about you in the air."

"I'll probably take a nice long nap. I didn't sleep so well last night without you next to me in the bed."

"Me, too. I tossed and turned most of the night. Hey, can you sneak a bottle or two of the wine on the plane when you come back?"

"I probably can."

"Great. Maybe a couple of bottles of that merlot that was so good. Then I won't feel like I missed so much."

Ravyn and Marc kissed at the back of her car. She held him tight. Marc pulled away first. "I need to check in."

"OK. Love you," Ravyn said.

"Love you, too."

As Ravyn left the PDK gates, a car passed her coming in. She couldn't be sure, but she thought the driver of the black Mercedes looked like Laura Lucas.

Ravyn drove back to Julie's house in Buckhead and Marc headed into the small terminal to check in for his flight to Napa County Airport, a small airport that catered to charter and private aircraft.

The pilot came out to greet Marc, taking his bag. "I'm Ryan Hays. I'm your captain on today's flight," the pilot said, introducing himself. "No flight attendant today."

"That's fine," Marc said, surprised at Ryan's young age. Was he even old enough to fly the plane? he wondered.

"But there's snacks and bottled water back in the cabin, so help yourself. There's a fully stocked bar, too."

"Even better."

"We're just waiting on my co-pilot and one more passenger," the pilot said.

"Oh, no," Marc replied. "I thought maybe Kyle told you. My fiancée couldn't make it."

"No, there's another woman coming. Kyle said so."

Marc was confused. Who else was coming on the trip? He looked over and saw Laura Lucas walking from the terminal toward the plane.

"Laura," Marc said under his breath. He said it almost as a swear.

Laura Lucas and Marc went way back. Back to his days when he was running LindMark Enterprises as its CEO. He'd hired Laura to be his public relations and marketing representative. At first, she'd kept their relationship very professional.

Then Laura had made her move on Marc. The next thing he knew they were sexual partners. And Laura liked to amp up their sexual encounters. They had made love behind a Midtown nightclub; in Piedmont Park; in a dark alley behind the High Museum; on a hiking trail in Stone Mountain.

Laura liked the thrill of public sex and nearly being caught. Marc got swept away by her dangerous nature. He could feel himself getting hard just thinking about that time.

"Hello, lover," Laura said with a sly smile as she approached him. "Where's your girlfriend? Did she ditch you already?"

"My fiancée, Laura," Marc said. "She couldn't make the trip."

"You're engaged? I'm surprised. Can't believe you'd want to be tied to that little mouse for an eternity. I hope you've got a divorce attorney on speed dial."

"Laura," Marc growled.

"And she's not here? That's too bad for her and good for me," Laura purred.

"Why are you even here?"

"Didn't Kyle tell you? I'm his new public relations and marketing representative."

"He did not tell me," Marc said. "I'm not happy about it."

"You don't have to be happy about it. I'm his new hire and I'm going out to help get some publicity for this little rinky dink winery. I'm going to get him some valuable, dollars and cents, results. Why are you going out?"

"I'm going to look over the operations. Make sure they are in order and running well."

"Well, give me a hand up, Marc," Laura said, extending her hand as she stepped on the stairs into the plane, an eight-passenger Cessna Citation.

Marc took Laura's hand and could immediately feel a spark between them. He was not looking forward to the flight. He planned to head to the well-stocked bar as soon as he could.

Marc was pleasantly surprised to find high-end liquor aboard Black Kat Investor's private jet. Marc drank scotch, a nice single malt, almost the entire flight. Laura sat across from him in the jet sipping white wine. Her short skirt rode up so he could see her smooth legs. He tried not to think about the time those legs were wrapped around his neck.

Laura asked him if he was staying at the B&B Kyle had suggested. He nodded. "Oh, that's great. I am, too. We can have dinner together," she said.

Marc shook his head no. He didn't want to be around Laura. He knew her wiles and whims. He didn't want to fall for that again.

"Oh, come on," Laura said. "You're not afraid to have dinner with me, are you? I know you, Marc. You wouldn't be rude to a woman."

"I'm not having dinner with you, Laura. We are not going to be spending time together. I'm sorry if that disappoints you."

"What disappoints me is your commitment to Ravyn. She's a mouse. She won't give you what you want, what you need."

"And you will?"

"Of course, I will," Laura purred, sliding over to sit in the seat next to him. "You know I will."

"No, Laura. You can never give me what I want. I want a real woman. A woman who won't play games the way you did. With you it was all a game, a sport. I need stability in my life and Ravyn gives me that."

Laura smiled her knowing smile. "You don't need Ravyn. You need someone exciting like me. You need to feel alive, Marc. I know you. You need me."

Laura gave Marc a wicked smile and tried to reach his crotch with her foot. "Want to join the mile-high club?"

"No, Laura," he said, batting her foot away. "Not with you."

"Too bad. I know Ravyn wouldn't even suggest doing that. She's a mouse."

Marc wouldn't even dignify Laura with an answer, even though he realized she was probably right. He spent the rest of the flight in silence, drinking scotch. He felt slightly drunk by the time they landed, nearly five hours later.

"Can you help me with my bags, Marc," Laura said after they landed. "And we'll share an Uber."

Laura hadn't even asked. It was a statement. Like she and Marc were going to spend the weekend together. Like she was running the show. He didn't want it this way. But she was right. It wasn't in him to be rude to her. And he hated that about himself.

They exited the terminal at Napa County Airport and Laura turned to Marc to get the Uber. He was irritated that she expected him to do everything for her, but he did and at last the Uber SUV arrived to take them to their B&B.

Laura settled into the back seat, but Marc sat sullen.

Laura leaned up to the Uber driver. "Are you a local? Can you recommend a good restaurant for dinner tonight?"

"I recommend Celadon," the driver said. "There is a nice patio and the weather is supposed to be excellent tonight."

"What kind of food is it?" Marc asked.

"Well, it's American, but it's really good," the driver said.

"Let's go there," Laura said. "Do we need to make reservations?"

"You probably should," the driver said.

Laura pulled out her cell phone and began searching for the restaurant. She punched at her phone and then announced to Marc they had reservations at 6 p.m. "I made the reservations early since I knew you'd be tired and on Eastern time, and you've been drinking."

Marc scowled at her. It was none of her business if he'd been drinking on the plane. Why was she assuming he'd be tired? Though he was beginning to feel a bit sleepy. He shouldn't have drunk so much.

"I'll be fine," he said, blankly. "I just want to get to the B&B and freshen up."

"Need some help freshening up?" Laura asked, coyly, placing her hand on Marc's arm.

Marc jerked his arm away. "Not from you, I don't."

Laura smiled knowingly. She was determined to get Marc into her bed this weekend.

Chapter 9

Ravyn was exhausted by the time she got into bed Friday night. Julie's girls were full of energy and wanted to play games, dress up, and by and large kept her occupied all night. Even when she'd gotten the girls to bed, they kept getting up, asking for water, a snack, another chapter in their chapter book.

Julie's husband Rob had gotten home shortly after 10 p.m. He'd texted Ravyn that he planned to head over to his office after Julie's surgery. He wanted to pick up some work that he could do over the weekend.

Julie's surgery had gone well, he'd reported earlier that day, to Ravyn's relief. Julie wasn't in much pain, he'd said, but she was pretty doped up. She wasn't up to talking and couldn't really text.

Instead, Ravyn had just texted Julie, wishing her well, and that she hoped she'd be coming home soon.

As Ravyn drifted off to sleep she vaguely thought she hadn't gotten a text from Marc after his flight or gotten a call from him. She assumed he'd landed safely. She contemplated getting up to text him, but sleep won out.

When Ravyn awoke Saturday morning to the sounds of little feet pounding down the hall, she quickly got up and pulled her robe over her T-shirt and sleep shorts. Lexie and Ashley loudly whispered at her shut bedroom door. "I don't hear anything," Lexie said. "She must still be asleep."

"Let's go watch TV," Ashley said.

"I'm up! I'm up!" Ravyn replied. "No TV. I'll fix breakfast."

Ravyn opened her door to two giggling girls. "What have you done?" Ravyn asked.

"Come see! Come see!" Ashley squealed. Each girl took a hand and pulled Ravyn down the hallway.

They opened Ashley's bedroom door and Ravyn saw handmade signs to welcome their mother home. Glitter and spilled glue littered the carpeted floor, however. Ravyn smiled, even though she wanted to shout about the mess.

Is this what having kids will be like? she wondered. Thank God, she and Marc weren't thinking of having kids soon. Although, to be fair, she'd never even asked him about their timeline for having children. She wanted to be married for at least a year before they even thought about kids.

"These are just beautiful," Ravyn said of their signs. "But you've made a bit of a mess. Lexie, go get a wet towel and Ashley get the vacuum cleaner. We need to get this cleaned up. We won't want your mom to see this mess."

The girls raced in different directions to collect the cleaning supplies. Ravyn held up one sign: Welcome Home, Mommy! Another said: We Love You!

The girls came back into the bedroom and Ravyn got Ashley working the vacuum while she scrubbed the glue embedded in the carpet. It wasn't coming out easily. Ravyn realized when she had kids they'd be in a bedroom with a hardwood or tiled floor. That would be much easier to clean.

Rob left for the hospital right after breakfast but promised to return around lunch so Ravyn could check on Felix.

It was well after noon before Ravyn was able to slip away to her house to check on her tomcat. She'd barely had a chance to shower that day. As soon as she got into her home she collapsed on the couch. She didn't realize how tired she was. How did Julie do this day after day?

It's no wonder Julie wanted to meet Ravyn for drinks so often. She needed adult conversation, Ravyn thought. And a break from her very active daughters. They really were good girls, though. Ravyn hadn't any reason to complain. They'd only gotten into a few arguments since she'd been there.

Whose turn was it to pick the cartoon they would watch after breakfast? Whose shirt was that? Whose turn was it to set the table? Ravyn had broken up an argument about hair ties of all things.

Felix purred and curled up next to her on the couch and before she knew it, she was asleep. Her phone rang an hour later.

"Hey, where are you?" Rob asked.

"Sorry, Rob, I fell asleep on the couch. I'll be back in just a few minutes. I've still got to clean out the litter box."

"OK. It's just I forgot a couple of documents at the office, so I need to go back."

"Give me 20 minutes."

"Great."

Ravyn hauled herself up to tend to Felix, sorry she wouldn't get to relax a little longer in her own house.

On her way back to Julie's house, Ravyn tried to call Marc, but it went to voicemail. "Hey, just wanted to make sure you're OK. I didn't hear from you after you landed. The girls are running me ragged. And funny thing, I thought I saw Laura Lucas pulling into PDK as I was leaving. She's not there is she? No, I'm sure she isn't. Sorry. My mind must be playing tricks on me. I'll try to call back tonight. Love you."

Ravyn pulled into Julie's Buckhead home and Rob walked out the front door to his car. Clearly, he'd been watching her from the front window so he could escape.

"I've decided it might be better if I just work a bit at the office tonight. It'll be quieter that way," he said as he opened his car door. "I hope you don't mind."

"No, no. That's fine," she said. "Will you go see Julie?"

"I just talked to her. They said she can be discharged tomorrow morning. I'll run by the hospital to see her before visiting hours are over."

Ravyn tried not to frown. Jesus, she was glad Rob wasn't her husband! Not even at his wife's bedside in the hospital. Not that she expected Marc would be holding her hand at her bedside every minute, but she thought Rob should be more attentive to Julie, given she'd just had abdominal surgery.

Ravyn was getting an eye-opening peek at Julie and Rob's relationship. She started to wonder how it had survived after Rob's infidelity. Ravyn wasn't so sure she'd be quite so forgiving if Marc ever cheated on her.

She was greeted at the front door with taped together banners welcoming Julie home. There was more glitter on the hardwood foyer floor. This time she could ask the girls to clean it up with a broom.

By the time that was done, Ravyn needed to get dinner started. Was it poor form to pour herself a glass of wine while she cooked? Well, if Julia Child could drink her way through her televised cooking classes, Ravyn could have a glass herself.

Ravyn reached into the tall kitchen cabinet and pulled down a pinot noir that was open. Perfect, Ravyn thought. A glass and a half in, Ravyn realized exactly how Julie coped with her busy family sometimes. Wine.

She called the girls to the dinner table. She'd fixed comfort food for the girls tonight: mac and cheese (although it was homemade and not from a box), chicken nuggets and green beans. Ravyn was thankful for the frozen nuggets. She giggled as she wondered if the pinot noir paired well with the nuggets.

"What's so funny, Auntie Ravyn?" Lexie asked.

Ravyn caught herself. "Oh, I was just thinking of a funny time I had with your mother. Can you think of some funny things you've done with her?"

"I can! I can!" Ashley said, raising her hand as if she were still in the classroom.

"No! I want to tell first!" Lexie shouted.

"Lexie, Ashley can go first," Ravyn said.

Lexie threw her fork on her plate, crossed her arms and scowled. Ravyn took another sip of wine.

"Lexie, you just have to wait your turn," Ashley scolded.

Ravyn could see Lexie was near tears, so she quickly added, "Ashley, just tell your story, please."

"Well, this one time, when we were little, Lexie and I played this game and hid in the store at Macy's in the clothes and Mommy couldn't find us. That was so funny!"

"That was the story I was going to tell!" Lexie said, bursting into tears.

Ravyn took a large sip of wine. Oh God! If her children ever did that, she'd be wild with fear! What if someone had kidnapped the girls?!

"Well, it might have been funny to you, but I'm sure your Mommy was frantic with fear for your safety, so you might want to rethink that game," Ravyn said, as coolly as she could.

"Yeah, Mommy was kind of mad, but it was funny," Ashley said, suddenly serious.

"See, you got us in trouble," Lexie said. "It was your idea!"

"Was not!"

"Was too!"

"Girls! Let's not argue. Let's finish our meal in peace," Ravyn said, pouring herself another glass of pinot noir. She was very glad she was staying over that Saturday night. She felt sure she'd be good and tipsy by the time she could corral the girls to bed.

She also wanted to call Marc. She hoped she wasn't going to be too drunk when she talked to him.

Marc and Laura met Robert Pierce Saturday morning for a tour of the winery. He planned to show them the grounds, and explain the art of winemaking, before showing Marc the records he kept of the winery.

Laura realized she'd be on her own after the tour. But she'd spied some shops on the way to the restaurant the night before, so she'd be able to keep herself occupied.

"Mr. Pierce, thanks for meeting with us this morning," Marc said, shaking Robert's hand.

"Please, it's Bobby. Mr. Pierce is my late father."

"Well, I'm Marc and this is Laura,"

Bobby looked down at their feet. "Did you bring any old boots or shoes you don't mind getting dirty?"

Laura laughed. "You're kidding, right?"

She dressed as she would to meet any client, a rust-colored blouse cut very low, showing off her ample cleavage, and her leopard print short skirt. She was also wearing leopard print Jimmy Choo stiletto heels, giving some height to her petite frame.

"This is a working farm, essentially," Bobby explained. "We don't have cows or pigs, but we do have tractors and other farm equipment. It can get pretty dusty when it's dry and muddy when it's wet. We've had rain recently so the ground is probably muddy. Let me see if I've got some spare boots for the both of you. Might be harder to find some for you, Laura. I have mostly men's boots."

Laura just frowned. "That's fine. I'll make do."

Bobby returned from a shed with two pair of large boots. He handed one pair to Marc and the other to Laura. "You might want to take those heels off and just wear these without any shoes on."

Laura made a face and tried to put her stilettos in the first boot, then the second. She tried walking and immediately fell over. Bobby caught her under her arms as she went sideways. His hands touched soft flesh.

Laura smirked as Bobby blushed, dropping his hands as Laura righted herself. She then sat on a nearby bench and removed both boots, then her shoes, reluctantly putting her bare feet in the boots. "I hope I don't get athlete's foot from these!"

The boots were too large for her, but Laura wasn't going to be left behind on the tour.

"Let's start out in the ATV to get out to the far end of the vineyards. We can walk around when we get there and I'll explain a bit about how we grow the grapes and the process of winemaking."

Bobby hopped in the driver's seat while Marc gave Laura a hand up into the passenger's seat before he climbed in the back.

Bobby drove slowly for about 40 minutes, talking about the grapes grown, what they were used for, the equipment they used to irrigate the vines when the winery didn't get enough rain.

When they arrived at their destination, Bobby hopped down and walked around to help Laura, who had already started to get out of the ATV. She slipped and put her hand out to catch herself, but her right boot was stuck fast in the mud and now her hand was filthy, too.

"I'm stuck!" she exclaimed.

"Let me help you," Bobby said. "Hold onto my arm and pull your leg up. Your boot might stay in the mud, but I'll get it out."

Laura pulled her foot as best she could, but her boot remained firmly in the ground. At least her foot was free. She clung to Bobby so she didn't fall back in the mud.

Laura could smell his musky sweat and the faint scent of soap. She noticed the eagle tattoo on his arm, just under his T-shirt sleeve, and the full tattoo sleeve on his opposite arm.

"Nice ink," she commented.

Bobby smiled shyly. "Got them after my father died. He wouldn't let us boys get any sort of tattoos when we were younger. Said those were for motorcycle gangs. Once he was gone I could do as I pleased."

Laura could sense Bobby's displeasure at her being there, but she felt herself get a little aroused by the moment. Maybe this trip wasn't going to be so bad after all.

Ravyn climbed into bed Saturday night, once again exhausted. This time she was also drunk. She picked up her phone to text Marc. She knew it was probably a bad idea to drunk text him, but she hadn't heard from him all day Saturday either.

She looked at her phone and squinted one eye, trying to remember what time it was in California. It was 10:30 p.m. in Atlanta, so it was 7:30 p.m. in Napa. It was OK to text him.

Hey, miss you. Haven't heard from you, so I hope you are there and OK.

Ravyn laid in the bed, drifting off to sleep, but about five minutes later, she heard the text message ping on her phone and she jerked awake.

Sorry I haven't called yet. The operations and books here are in a bit of a mess. At dinner now. Can I call you later?

Honey, the girls have worn me out again. And I've had lots of wine. I'm in bed. Talk to you tomorrow then. Love you.

Love you, too.

Marc looked up from his phone at Laura Lucas. She'd insisted they try a different restaurant tonight. After all, she'd said, this was a business expense.

"So, does the mouse miss you?"

"Stop it, Laura."

"Why isn't she here again?"

"I already told you. Her friend is in the hospital for surgery and needed help looking after her children."

"Ugh!" Laura said, shaking her shoulders, as if the thought of children was revolting. "I never want kids. Snotty, germ-filled rug rats."

"That's why we'd never be a couple, Laura. I want children."

"You? I figured you for the bachelor playboy. I don't see you as a father."

"Why not?"

"You never said a kind word about your own father when we were together. You always complained about him."

"That's not true," Marc protested. "I may not have gotten along with my father at times, but I still respect him."

"Respect him, yes, but can you say you love him?" Laura asked, pointedly.

Marc started to protest again, then stopped. He wasn't sure he could say he loved his father. Marc's father was a hard man to love, in Marc's opinion. Edward Linder hadn't made loving him easy.

"What are you ordering?" Marc asked.

"You're changing the subject."

"Maybe I am. Just drop it, Laura."

"OK, so I'm thinking about the mussels. And I'd get a white wine to go with that."

"So, I need to get either seafood or chicken to share your wine."

"No, you get what you want. We can always bring the wine back to the B&B and finish it there."

"Hmm, a steak looks good. And they have a really good Cabernet here."

"Well, get that and we can just bring the bottles back with us, unless we finish the bottles here."

"I'm not sure I'm drinking an entire bottle of Cabernet here," Marc said.

"You never know. You might enjoy the evening more than you expect. Besides, we're taking an Uber back."

Laura and Marc downloaded into small talk, then stopped talking all together when the food arrived. Marc wasn't comfortable around Laura anymore. He felt like he always needed to keep his guard up.

For her part, Laura sat in silence trying to figure out how to seduce Marc. She'd been attracted to him once. His millions made him more attractive. But it just burned her ass that Marc had proposed to Ravyn. Ravyn! That goodie two shoes. Marc was definitely settling, in her opinion.

Hell, Laura thought the guy that operated Star 1 was a better sexual prospect. Bobby Pierce was definitely cute, with that eagle tattoo on his upper arm and another arm with a full tattoo sleeve. It had roses, skulls and more that she'd like to run her fingers over. And his neatly trimmed goatee. She wondered what that would feel like between her thighs. She gave a little shudder of delight at the thought.

"Everything OK?" Marc asked.

"Huh?" Marc's question pulled Laura from her reverie. First things first. Her sights were set on Marc. She'd think about Bobby later.

Marc and Laura ended up finishing their bottles of wine and sharing an Uber back to their B&B. Laura attempted to invite Marc in for a nightcap.

"Nightcap? Are you pilfering the sherry at this place?" "No. I got a bottle of the scotch you like today while shopping. The Macallan, 12-year, right? Come in and have a nightcap with me."

"I can't. I've gotta get up early and work out why those books don't look quite right tomorrow. Bobby's got a good head for business, but I don't understand some of the numbers. The wine was enough tonight."

"Come on, one won't hurt."

"No thanks, Laura. Good night."

Laura shut her bedroom door and brooded. This was going to be more difficult than she thought.

Ravyn woke up Sunday to the sound of little feet down the hallway, but this time Lexie and Ashley didn't stand outside her door and stage whisper loudly. They burst through the door and threw themselves on her bed.

Ravyn's head pounded from too much wine the night before. She needed coffee in the worst way.

"Hey girls! Good morning!" she said, trying to sound merrier than she felt.

"Good morning, Auntie Ravyn! Mommy's coming home today!"

"Yes, she is. Now you know you'll have to be a bit quieter when she gets home. She'll be tired from her hospital stay. Why don't you practice being more quiet right now? Can you do that for Auntie?"

Lexie put her finger to her lips and walked out of the bedroom. Then Ashley did the same. But then they ran down the hallway and down the stairs. It sounded like a herd of elephants.

Ravyn pulled her pillow over her head. She desperately wanted to sleep some more, but she knew she'd have to get up. Lord knows Julie's husband Rob wasn't going to take care of his daughters' breakfasts.

Ravyn remembered she'd promised the girls chocolate chip pancakes that morning as a treat. She had a feeling she'd be making them from scratch unless she found premade pancake mix in the pantry.

Dear God, Ravyn thought, please let Julie have premade pancake mix!

Ravyn pulled on her robe and plodded down the stairs to the kitchen. She had no idea where Ashely and Lexie were, but she loaded the coffee maker and hit start.

The aroma of the coffee almost made Ravyn weep. She wished she could just start an IV and inject the coffee straight into her veins.

She found pancake mix in the pantry — premade! — and then the mini chocolate chips in the refrigerator. Ravyn got the gas griddle in the middle of the range top good and hot before she poured out the golden batter with the chips mixed in.

"Girls! Wash your hands! Pancakes are about ready!"

Ravyn didn't hear any footsteps. She was going to have to use her mama Julie voice. "Girls! Now!" she shouted. She'd heard Julie use that tone on more than one occasion.

Ravyn heard footsteps into the half bath in the hallway, heard water running, then footsteps running into the kitchen.

"Plates are right here," she said, pointing to her left. "Get your plate and I'll add the hot pancakes. I've got bacon in the microwave, too. There's orange juice and milk on the table."

"Where's Daddy? Is he coming to breakfast?" Lexie asked. "Can I have toast?"

"I'm not sure where your Daddy is, and yes, you can have toast," Ravyn said, pushing two slices of bread into the toaster.

"Daddy!" Lexie screamed. "Breakfast is ready!"

Ravyn's head hurt more in this chaos. She reached for more coffee as Rob padded into the kitchen, scratching his belly. The master bedroom was on the main floor. She wasn't sure how he didn't hear all the noise or smell the smells of breakfast before now.

"Coffee," he said. It wasn't a request; it was a command.

Ravyn handed over a cup as Rob filled it from the pot.

"What's for breakfast?" Rob asked.

"Chocolate chip pancakes, bacon, orange juice, milk, and toast," Ravyn replied.

"Any pancakes without chocolate chips?"

"No, sorry."

"Julie usually makes a separate batter for me."

"Sorry, I didn't know that," Ravyn said, rather irritated.

"It's OK. You didn't know."

"What time are you picking Julie up?"

"I can't get her before 11 a.m. The surgeon is supposed to do his rounds and give her the OK before she can leave."

"OK. I'm just anxious to have her home."

"Had enough of the Montgomery household?" Rob asked, smiling.

"Well, you do have a challenging household, that's for sure."

"Just wait, Ravyn. Children change everything."

"Well, Marc and I plan to wait. We're not ready for that."

"Julie and I weren't ready either. But, Whoop! There it is!" Rob said, echoing the Tag Team song.

Ravyn looked over at Ashley, who was buttering another piece of toast with way too much butter. Was Rob saying Ashley was unexpected?

"I know what you're thinking, Ravyn," he said, as if reading her mind. "I wouldn't trade my daughters for anything, but we didn't expect to be parents so soon after we got married. Life just happens."

Rob left shortly after breakfast to stay with Julie before her discharge and Ravyn got the girls into their showers to get squeaky clean for their mother's arrival. She didn't want Julie to think she couldn't get her daughters presentable after her hospital stay, after all!

Ravyn realized she was going to spend Sunday with the family. There was no way Julie was going to be ready for this chaos. As the girls bathed, Ravyn grabbed a quick shower. She honestly wanted to stay in there for an hour, or until the hot water ran out. Ravyn was so tired.

Marc awoke, finally on Pacific time. He'd not slept well since he'd landed in California. He was missing Ravyn and leery of

Laura. He ached for Ravyn's body in the king bed of the B&B. Many times that night he'd thrown his arm over, but Ravyn's warm soft body wasn't there.

He threw his legs over the bed and grabbed his phone. He knew Ravyn should be up by now on Sunday.

Hey, how's it going at Julie's house? Is she home from the hospital?

Marc got no response, so he put down his phone and headed to the shower. He was also ready for some coffee.

When he got out of the shower there was a response from Ravyn.

OMG. I am so tired. Julie should be here any moment, but I'm glad I opted to stay today.

I'm glad you are there if it's that tough.

Jesus, I'm glad I'm marrying you and not Rob.

???, Marc texted, confused.

He's leaving me to the girls. Not involved AT ALL.

Sorry.

Please tell me you'll be involved with our children.

Marc paused. He wanted to be completely involved with his children. He didn't want to be like his father, always working late at the office and acting like his children were a burden, not a blessing.

Of course. I completely want to be a part of their lives.

You say that now.

NO. I want to be a part of our children's lives. My father wasn't there for me. I don't want to be like him.

Ravyn was shocked. Marc had never said his father wasn't part of his life. She knew he and his father didn't get along well, but this seemed to be deep seated anger.

OK. After this weekend I'll want all the help I can get with kids. I don't know how Julie does it. I needed lots of wine.

Wish you were here. Lots of good wine. Love you

Love you, too. Don't forget to bring back home some of that good wine for me.

I want to have children with you, Ravyn.

Ravyn paused for a moment before she responded. Julie's girls were a handful. Was she ready for that?

I want children with you, too, Ravyn answered, truthfully.

Did I tell you Laura is here?

Ravyn needed a moment to process what Marc had just texted.

What?

Laura's here. Kyle hired her as his PR person.

What? She's there with you?

I know. I don't like it either.

Do you see her often?

Marc didn't want to lie to Ravyn, so he tried to play down how much time he was spending with Laura.

Not that much. She's doing her PR thing and I'm doing my business thing.

Should I be worried? Ravyn texted.

Absolutely not. I'm engaged to you. I love you. Don't you forget that.

Julie arrived home later Sunday, grateful that Ravyn was staying to help with the girls. Julie still just wanted to sleep, but her daughters wanted their mother's undivided attention.

"Let's let your Mommy rest for a bit. We can do that puzzle with the kitties on it," Ravyn told the girls, herding them out of Julie's bedroom. As Ravyn closed the door behind her she could see Julie mouth "Thank you."

Ravyn again fixed dinner that night, taking a tray to Julie in the bedroom. Ravyn desperately wanted to tell Julie that Laura was in California with Marc and she was a bit worried. Not that she didn't trust Marc. She just didn't trust Laura.

But now wasn't the time. Julie was propped up on lots of pillows but needed some help to get up to use the bathroom. Then she needed Ravyn's help to get her settled again.

"I'm sorry you are in so much pain," Ravyn said.

"I have some pain pills. I really don't want to take them if I don't have to," Julie said.

"Well if you are in pain you should take them."

"I've got synthetic hormones to take from now on, too, since I'll be in menopause," Julie said, a tear rolling down her face. "I'm nearly 40 and in menopause. That just doesn't seem right."

Ravyn sat closer to her friend on the bed, wrapping her arm gently around her. "I'm sorry. I know this is really hard on you."

"I just don't know what it will mean for me, and for me and Rob," Julie said.

"What do you mean?"

"You know, menopause makes everything drier. Down there. I've heard some older women complain that sex becomes painful and they don't want to do it anymore. Rob will never go for that."

"Won't the hormones help? With the down below business?"

"I hope so. But my doctor said I can't stay on them forever. Women taking hormones have had problems, like strokes and blood clots."

"Oh no. What will you do?"

"We might have to find an alternative. We might have to go to one of those sex shops and find some good lubricant," Julie whispered.

Ravyn burst out laughing. She could just see her and Julie in wigs and dark glasses pawing over the various lubricants at a sex shop, like the Love Shack in Atlanta. "You know Julie, I think they sell lubricant at the grocery store."

Julie's eyes got wide. "I can't let my neighbors see me buying that at the grocery store! The cashiers know me by name!"

By the time Ravyn returned to her home late Sunday night she was worn out again. She'd played several games of Uno with Ashley, Lexie and Julie around Julie's bed. She could tell Ashley and Lexie were working against her when they kept laying their Draw 2 cards and Ravyn ended up with a fistful of cards.

After Ravyn got the girls to bed, Ravyn and Julie had had a small glass of wine. Julie promised she was not taking a pain pill that night.

Ravyn then rolled her suitcase to her Honda and headed back to her Garden Hills home. She was glad she would be sleeping in her own bed that night.

But Ravyn tossed and turned in the master bed. When she finally fell asleep, she dreamt of Marc in Laura's arms. Then she dreamt of Marc naked and telling Laura he didn't love Ravyn. Then Ravyn dreamt she was making love to Marc, but he called out Laura's name. It was a confusing, restless night.

Chapter 10

Despite his objections, Marc and Laura had dinner together every night of their trip, always at a different restaurant near Star 1. On the final night of Marc and Laura's stay, Bobby Pierce wanted to show off the event space, hosting a dinner with a private chef and some special vintages.

"Now this is a space I can work with," Laura said as she saw the setup. "Why didn't Bobby show me this space upfront? I mean I'm trying to get some good PR for this place and he hides this gem from me."

"Didn't we see this on the tour? It had equipment stored in here, didn't it?"

Marc expressed sympathy, but he had his own worries about Star 1. It wasn't a poor investment for Black Kat Investors, per se, but wine production was low this year and some of the vines had been infected with a bacterium. Most of the vines could be treated, others would have to be replanted entirely. And replanted vines would take at least three years before there was good grape production.

Marc read online that even with grapes able to produce wine in those three years, it might be two more years for a good vintage. Star 1 vineyard might not be profitable in the five years Black Kat Investors had wanted.

Marc would write up a report tomorrow on the flight back to Atlanta. He knew Kyle Quitman had done his due diligence before the purchase. Given some of the problems he'd discovered, Marc was puzzled why Black Kat Investors hadn't uncovered the issues he'd found.

Bobby seemed knowledgeable about how to run the winery. And some of the issues were out of his control. But Star 1 was going to need more capital, in Marc's opinion. He wasn't sure Black Kat was ready for that.

Laura was seated next to Marc at dinner. "So, you're leaving tomorrow?" she asked.

"Aren't you?"

"No. I've decided to stay another week. I want to see if I can get a photographer here to shoot this space, see if I can get some publicity in wedding magazines. This place would be perfect for weddings, bachelorette parties, baby showers. I need to hire some actors, too. Need to get all that set up, like yesterday."

Marc couldn't suppress his grin and relief. He wouldn't have to fly back with Laura.

"Well, you don't have to look so happy about it," she snapped.

"Oh, Laura, I'm not going to lie and say my flight home won't be a pleasure without you. It will. But where are you staying? I thought the B&B was booked."

"So, you want to know where I'll be? There's been a cancelation for the weekend and I got it. Why don't you stay with me? It's just one bedroom though. But I'd make it worth your while. Just like old times. I'd make you forget about your mouse."

"Not a chance, Laura," Marc barked. "You sabotaged my business and nearly cost me my relationship with Ravyn. You won't do it again."

Laura tried not to let Marc see her shock and hurt. "There's no need to be mean about it. Let's just try to be civil and enjoy the evening tonight," Laura said, forcing a smile and pouring him another glass of wine.

Marc thought she looked like the cat who was about to catch the canary. He suddenly felt like he'd sprouted a tiny beak and little yellow feathers.

Marc and Laura walked up the stairs of the bed and breakfast, Laura carrying a nearly full bottle of wine and two stemmed wine glasses.

She'd cornered a male server in the supply closet, giving him a quick blow job and liberating the bottle of wine. The glasses she grabbed off the bar.

"Planning to meet someone tonight? There might be a waiter still cleaning up at the party," Marc said, not unkindly.

"No, silly, I'm inviting myself into your room for a nightcap."

"No, Laura. I've had enough to drink tonight and so have you."

"Keeping track of how much I drink? How very sweet of you."

Marc opened the door to his room and Laura pushed her way in. "Come on. Just one drink. I don't want to finish the bottle alone. Then I'll leave. I promise. And you shall remain unsullied and chaste."

"You promise?" he asked, raising an eyebrow. He threw his key card on the table by the TV.

"Scout's honor," Laura said, raising two fingers.

"That's three fingers for Scout's honor, Laura."

"It is? How do you know? Were you the good little Boy Scout?"

"I was."

"I didn't know that about you, but I can see it." Laura placed the wine glasses on the small table in the corner of the bedroom and poured the rich Cabernet she'd nabbed from the server. She still saw the look of sweaty bliss on his face after the blow job. The catering staff wasn't getting this bottle for their clean up meal tonight.

An hour and a half later, the bottle was empty.

"Laura, you said you'd leave without a fuss," Marc said, standing up.

"I don't think I said I'd go without a fuss, but I will go," she said. She stood up and leaned into Marc and kissed him. He didn't intend to, but he ended up kissing her back. Then he pulled away.

"Laura, you can see yourself out," he said, heading to the bathroom.

As Marc's back was to her, she swiped the key card to his room. "I'll leave, Marc," she said under her breath. "But I'll be back."

Marc splashed cold water on his face and looked in the mirror. He shook his head and tried not to think about Laura's kiss. He felt guilty. He needed to get Laura out of his mind and out of his life forever.

He stripped down to his boxers and got into bed. He opened the window near the bed and felt a cool breeze. The breeze felt good. After all the wine he'd had that evening, he fell asleep quickly and deeply.

Laura sat in her darkened bedroom wearing her sheer black silk lingerie. She was waiting until she could be sure Marc would be asleep. His key card felt hot in her hand.

Laura looked down at her phone. The time read 2 a.m. She quietly went to her door and slipped out of her bedroom, heading to his room.

She paused to listen at the door and heard nothing. She didn't want to be caught by anyone in the hallway, or by him when she opened his door.

She used her phone to light the key card lock and slipped it in. Laura heard the click and held her breath. She slowly opened the door and slipped into Marc's room.

She used her phone to light her way and felt a chill from the open window. Goose flesh rose up on her skin and her nipples became erect.

Laura smiled. That would actually help in her quest. She peered into the darkness and spotted Marc's phone at the bedside table near him. She walked around the bed and got it.

But she didn't know Marc's password. What could it be? she wondered. She carefully typed in the numeric numbers for RAVYN and it unlocked. Laura smirked at how easy it was to guess his password.

"Jackass," she said under her breath.

Laura needed to be careful as she crept around the room, but she remembered Marc was a sound sleeper. With Marc's phone unlocked, Laura returned to the empty side of the bed.

Did she dare to slip into the bed and take the photo with his phone or with hers? She'd need to take the photo with her phone. It wouldn't make sense for Marc to take a photo of himself asleep in bed.

Laura decided to chance at least sitting on the edge of the bed. She pulled down one strap of her lingerie, exposing her left breast. She licked her fingers and gave her nipple a little tug, making sure it was erect. She wasn't sure it would be visible in the darkened bedroom.

Laura turned her phone camera to a selfie, stuck her chest out and made sure Marc was visible in the bed behind her. Snap went the phone's camera. Marc stirred and Laura held her breath.

Marc rolled over, almost touching her. She took one more photo, then tiptoed into the bathroom.

Laura used her phone's light to find Ravyn's name in Marc's contacts, punched Ravyn's number into her phone and sent the photo of her and Marc in the bed. "Enjoyed my time with your boyfriend," she texted.

Laura turned Marc's phone off, locking it and returned it to the bedside table. She then placed his key card on the table by the TV where she'd found it. She gingerly crept out of his bedroom and smiled a smug smile.

"I hate you, Ravyn," she hissed as she returned to her room. "He was the best thing that ever happened to me. He should have been mine."

Ravyn awoke around 6 a.m. Wednesday, hearing her phone's alarm. She groped for her phone on the nightstand and saw there was a message from an unknown Atlanta number. It had been sent very early that morning.

Ravyn looked at her phone, then screamed. The photo was blurry, but she could definitely make out a nearly naked Laura Lucas and a dim view of Marc in bed with her. The message read "Enjoyed my time with your boyfriend."

Ravyn couldn't breathe. What was happening? Laura was in bed with Marc! Ravyn felt like she was suffocating. All the air had left her lungs.

She began to cry, holding the phone to her chest. Ravyn felt like she was having a heart attack. She gulped for air and sobbed. How could Marc do this to her? He'd lied to her. He was with her! He'd slept with her!

Ravyn didn't know what to do, where to go. She couldn't stay in Marc's house. She couldn't face Marc. She couldn't see his guilty face, or worse, what if he acted like he wasn't guilty? Like nothing had happened?

She texted the only person she felt she could talk to: Julie.

Julie. Are you up? Marc's cheated on me!

Ravyn had to wait a few moments before Julie responded.

What are you talking about? Marc's in California, right?

Laura is there, too. He slept with her.

He told you that?

He didn't have to. Laura sent me this.

Ravyn sent the photo to Julie.

OMG. I'm calling you.

Julie called Ravyn and heard her crying.

"I can't believe he slept with her! He slept with her!"

"Are you sure he did? This is a very dark photo."

"She's in his bed! That's him!"

"When is he coming back? Maybe there's an explanation."

"He's coming back tonight. I'm supposed to pick him up at PDK. What explanation could he give? What will he explain? How he fucked Laura? No. I can't talk to him. I can't be here when he comes back."

"Where will you go?"

"I don't know, but I can't stay here. I can't be here in Atlanta. Maybe I'll go to South Carolina. But he'll probably call my parents. Julie, I don't know if I can marry him."

"Calm down, Ravyn. Calm down."

"How can I calm down? He cheated on me!"

"Ravyn," Julie said calmly. "I happen to know how it feels to be cheated on."

Ravyn went silent. "I'm sorry," she said, gulping for air. "I didn't know it would feel this bad."

"Listen, how about this. Rob, me and the girls were supposed to go to Cabo San Lucas over Memorial weekend. We booked it through a travel agency and got a great rate on a condo. But with my surgery, we couldn't go. It's all paid for. We prepaid months ago. We also didn't get our money back," Julie said with disgust. "I bet you can switch my ticket for your name and go."

"Where's Cabo San Lucas? Oh, I don't really care. It could be on the moon, for all I care. I just need to get away."

"It's not on the moon. It's in Mexico. On the Pacific Coast."

"Really? I'd need my passport, right?"

"Be quick about it. The flight leaves this afternoon. Call my travel agent and switch my ticket for your name."

Ravyn thought about it, then said, "I'm going. I'll call work and say I have the flu. Oh! But what do I do about Felix?"

"Felix? What about Marc? What happens when he gets home and you aren't here?"

"Screw him. I don't care what happens to him."

"I don't believe you. You love Marc. Let him explain."

"Explain what? So, he can lie to me? I just need to get away, Julie. I just need to think. Alone."

"OK. Pack a bikini or two. The resort looks gorgeous. I'll send you a link. And leave your front door key under the mat. Ashley and Lexie would love to come over to play with Felix."

Ravyn was fastening her seat belt on an airplane at Hartsfield-Jackson Atlanta International Airport about an hour before Marc was to land back in Atlanta.

Marc had tried to text and call Ravyn before he'd left California, but she didn't respond and his calls went to voicemail. That seemed odd to him, but he tried not to worry. Maybe Ravyn was busy with work. Marc was looking forward to being home and having the holiday weekend with Ravyn.

He landed around 7:30 p.m. and was surprised Ravyn wasn't there. He'd texted his landing time. Where was she? he wondered.

Marc began to worry. It wasn't like Ravyn to be late or not call or text. Had she been in an accident?

After waiting about 45 minutes, he called Julie. He hoped he wasn't calling too late.

"Hi Julie, do you know where Ravyn is? She was supposed to pick me up. She's not here and I'm worried."

"I believe she's on her way to Mexico, Marc."

"What? What do you mean? She's supposed to be picking me up at PDK."

"Marc, what happened between you and Laura in Napa?"

Marc paused, puzzled by Julie's question. Did she know about the kiss? No, she couldn't know about that.

"Nothing happened. Why?"

"Ravyn sent me this picture." Julie sent the photo of Laura and Marc in his bed.

Marc stood in stunned silence. When the hell was this taken? Marc turned ashen.

"What the fuck? How? That fucking bitch!" Marc shouted. "Julie, nothing happened! I swear! I'm not sure when this photo was taken, but I have an idea. My God! Laura sent this to Ravyn? Jesus! Where is Ravyn? Tell me, Julie!"

Marc paced back and forth in the small PDK terminal. The woman at the desk looked up at him, hearing him shout into the phone.

"Marc, she's on her way to Cabo San Lucas. She is staying at the condo Rob and I were planning to stay in. But my surgery prevented us from going."

"Tell me the name of the condo. I've got to get there. I've got to explain."

"How will you get there?"

"I've got to call Kyle's pilot. Maybe he can take me."

Julie gave Marc the name of the condo and resort. Marc scribbled it down on a piece of scrap paper. Marc immediately called Ryan, hoping he could fly him to Cabo San Lucas.

"Hey, Marc, did you leave something on the plane?" Ryan asked. "I can get it for you tomorrow."

"Ryan, can you fly me to Mexico tonight?"

"What? Mexico? Why do you want to go to Mexico? Hey, but no. I can't. I'm on my flight rest. Plus, I can't fly you anywhere without Kyle's OK. And it's expensive to put this plane in the air, especially that far."

"I'll call Kyle, see if he'll allow it. I'll pay for the flight and your time. When can you fly?"

"Not until tomorrow afternoon, maybe longer, since I'd have to file a flight plan."

"OK, I'll call Kyle and you make the flight plan."

"Sure thing. Can you tell me what's going on?"

"Laura Lucas is what's going on. She sent my fiancée a photo that looks, well, compromising. I'm sure my fiancée now has a very wrong idea and she ran off to Mexico today. I need to get to her," Marc paused, breathing heavily. "I just need to get to her."

"OK, I'll see what I can do on my end," Ryan said.

Kyle was in Texas, Central time, so Marc knew he could call him. Marc talked fast, his words rushing out, trying to explain what had happened. What Laura had done.

"Kyle, you really should reconsider hiring Laura," Marc said. "She's trouble. She'll cause you trouble, too."

"I didn't hire her, Marc," Kyle replied.

"What? She said you hired her."

"Not yet, I haven't. She's on a retainer. If she does well and gets solid publicity for the winery, then she gets a contract. I'll be sure she never does this again."

"Kyle, no disrespect, but I doubt you can stop Laura Lucas from doing anything. I doubt anyone can."

"Listen, I'll authorize this flight. I can tell you're upset and I really like Ravyn. Amy and I both do."

"Thank you, Kyle. I will pay you back."

"Damn straight you will. I'll text Ryan and let him know to take you to Mexico. Do you have your passport?"

"I'll need to go home to get it. Right now, I'm stranded at PDK. Ravyn didn't pick me up because she went to Mexico. I'll get an Uber. Thank you, Kyle. I owe you one."

"I won't let you forget it," he said, trying to kid Marc. "And don't worry. It will be alright."

Marc sincerely hoped it would be alright. For the first time that night, he felt like he could breathe, that his world wasn't falling apart.

Chapter 11

Ravyn landed at the Los Cabos International Airport and took a shuttle to the Grand Solmar at Rancho San Lucas. The Montgomerys had gotten an all-inclusive package and Ravyn planned to take full advantage of it.

The front desk clerk strapped a red waterproof wristband on her right wrist.

"Please, keep this on for your entire stay," the clerk said. "The staff will scan your wrist for all purchases with an RFID scanner. If you lose it, there will be a replacement fee."

Ravyn nodded before she grabbed her bag and turned toward the elevator.

She checked into her room, which was a grand studio, dropping her bag on the sofa. The small suite was meant to sleep Julie and her husband in the king bed, with their daughters sharing a queen bed. Ravyn smiled thinking this studio suite was bigger than her old condo in Midtown Atlanta.

Julie had emailed the vacation itinerary to Ravyn right before Ravyn had gotten on the flight. Julie had booked a spa treatment while Rob was planning on golfing. Ravyn wouldn't mind taking Julie's spa appointment, but she was not going to golf. She didn't know how or have clubs.

Then she looked more closely. Rob was also scheduled for a golf lesson. Hmm. Maybe she'd check that out. Maybe she'd go ahead and take the golf lesson. Surely the lesson would include some clubs she could borrow.

The resort had a fitness center, pools, several pool-side bars, including a swim-up bar, and several restaurants. Ravyn was glad she'd packed a couple of bikinis.

She grabbed her key card and decided to check out the resort, wandering in to see two of the restaurants and down to the pool. She then checked out the lagoon bar, the tide bar and sunset bar. There was even a little outdoor bar and grill.

Tourists were everywhere, sunning on chaise lounges near the pools. Ravyn immediately went back to her room and put on her bikini and sheer coverup. She slung her beach bag over her shoulder. It was time to soak up some sun.

She went back to one of the pools and asked a passing waiter if any chairs were free. The young blond man looked at her wristband and said she could choose any open one she could find. It was included with her package.

"I'm Sandy, by the way," he said, with a distinctive Australian accent. "Would you like a cocktail? It's included in your package as well. Your wristband is red. All-inclusive."

"Sandy, where are you from?" Ravyn asked.

"Brisbane, Queensland, Australia," he replied. "Have you been there?"

"No, but I went to a cooking school in Italy a couple of years ago and one of my fellow classmates was from Australia."

Sandy smiled. "That's great. Would you like a cocktail? There's a two-for-one special."

"Don't I have the all-inclusive deal?"

"Oh right. You do. But I can still bring you two drinks. Really, as many as you want."

"I think two will be fine. What do you recommend?"

"We have a Chardonnay, a Cabernet Sauvignon, a rose, or a mimosa. But our margaritas are very popular."

"Is there an appetizer menu? I'd better eat something too. I'm hungry."

Sandy produced a small bar menu. Ravyn chose the calamari and two glasses of rose but asked that the glasses be brought one at a time. As she waited for her food and drinks, she slathered on sunblock.

She was glad she'd thought to grab a spare bottle of sunscreen from when she'd been to Lake Lanier last Memorial Day weekend. The sunscreen came out thick and rather greasy. Ravyn thought maybe she'd have to buy a new bottle from the gift shop.

Sandy returned about five minutes later with her first glass of rose, then 15 minutes later with her fried calamari.

"Be careful, it's very hot," Sandy warned. "I just need to scan your wristband."

Ravyn held up her wrist and Sandy used an RFID scanner that was clipped to the waistband of his white uniform shorts. "It's how we keep track of the food and beverage in the inclusive packages. Are you here by yourself?"

"I am. Kind of a nice getaway. A honeymoon for one."

"Honeymoon for one? Is your husband here with you? Or maybe he's not."

"No, there is no husband. There's a boyfriend or *was* a boyfriend. It's complicated. I was just being funny. Or trying to be funny, anyway."

Sandy gave her a quizzical look, before asking, "What is your name?"

"Ravyn."

"Like the bird?" Sandy asked.

"Yes, like the bird. But it's spelled a little differently." She then spelled out her name.

"Say, I get off at 5 p.m. I'd be glad to show you around the resort. I can even show you some of Cabo," Sandy said.

"Thanks, but I'm fine for this evening," Ravyn responded. She had just run away from Marc. She had no interest in interacting with Sandy.

"Why don't I meet you for dinner. You don't want to eat alone. We'll eat right here at the resort. It's all free with your package. Anica is very good. There's even a vegan menu if you are vegan."

"I'm not vegan."

"No worries, then. I'll tell you what, I'll make a reservation for 8:30 and we can go there."

"Oh, you don't have to," Ravyn started to say.

"I insist. And if I don't put in the reservation we won't get in tonight. The resort is booked this weekend. What room are you in?" he asked.

Ravyn was not going to give out her room number to a man she just met by the pool. "Let's meet there at 8:30."

"Well. here's my phone number in case you get lost," Sandy said, producing a small business card out of his white uniform's shirt pocket.

Ravyn took it and read the name: Sandy King and saw the phone number beside it. This man is very smooth, she thought.

Ravyn finished her calamari and her first glass of rose and Sandy immediately took away her dirty dishes and returned with her second glass of rose.

Ravyn was going to have to be careful. In this heat the wine was going to her head. She rolled over onto her stomach, leaving her glass half full.

Sandy returned a few moments later. "Do you need me to apply more sunscreen? Your shoulders and back look like they are getting burned."

"Oh! I don't want to get burned on my first day here!"

"Here, let me help," he said, taking the sunscreen bottle from her and pouring an amount in his hand. He then began to stroke the lotion onto her shoulders and down her back.

At first, Ravyn tensed up when Sandy touched her, but his strong strokes down her back were soothing. His hands worked down to the small of her back and rested on her waist. She could almost feel herself falling asleep.

"Hey, don't go to sleep or you will burn," Sandy said.

Ravyn's eyes flew open and she started to stand. "I think it's the wine. Maybe I should return to my room for a nap. I'm tired from my flight."

"Where's home?"

"Atlanta, Georgia. In the States," Ravyn said as she gathered up her coverup, sandals and bag with her phone and sunglasses. She threw the sunscreen bottle in the bag as well.

"I know where Atlanta is," Sandy said.

"You do?"

"We have tourists from all over," he answered.

Ravyn picked up the half glass of rose and finished it, handing the empty glass back to Sandy. "Thanks for the food and drinks."

"Hey, you've got the premier all-inclusive package. Take advantage of it. But I'll see you tonight, right?"

"Yes. I'll see you at Anica at 8:30."

Ravyn returned to her suite, showered, then took a nap. She'd set her phone's alarm for 7 so she'd be ready for dinner, but had trouble rousing herself from sleep. She didn't realize the time change would affect her so much. She realized it was also the stress of the day.

When her alarm sounded on her phone, she fumbled for it. She could see Marc had tried to call and text. She was glad she'd turned off the phone's ringer.

I've seen the photo, one text said. **I DID NOT SLEEP WITH LAURA.** There were also several voicemails, all from Marc.

You bastard, she texted back. Ravyn then turned off her phone and wouldn't respond to anything else he sent. She still felt sick when she thought of that photo with him and a semi-nude Laura. It sure *looked* like he slept with Laura.

She got up and dressed, deciding on a light pink sundress with a dusky rose shawl. She strapped on a pair of nude-colored sandals and left her suite. She wanted to walk on the beach before she met Sandy for dinner.

Ravyn slipped off her sandals and walked barefoot in the surf. She was lost in thought, thinking of Marc and Laura, but also trying to quiet her mind. She walked the short part of the beach in front of the resort a couple of times. Rather than the waves calming her, they seemed to unsettle her.

Ravyn turned back to the resort, weaving her way through more and more tourists. There were native men and women hawking some jewelry, bottled water and other wares in between the hotel guests.

Suddenly, Ravyn felt a hand on her arm and jumped back. A small, older native man held Ravyn in her grip.

"You are in danger, miss," the old man said.

"What?" asked Ravyn, alarmed. She looked from side to side to see if she was in danger.

"You feel betrayed, but you are threatened by another," he said. "Come I will read the cards for you."

Ravyn felt herself pulled along to a small alcove, where the man made her sit down in front of a small wooden table. A deck of tarot cards was on the table. The man sat opposite Ravyn.

"Please, calm your mind," he said.

"What is your name?"

"Pablo," the man said. "And yours?"

"Ravyn."

"Such a beautiful name for a troubled woman. What worries you, my lovely friend?"

Ravyn wasn't sure why, but she began to tell the tarot reader she'd had a falling out with her fiancé.

The man began to shuffle the deck of tarot cards. He had Ravyn pull out four of them, face down.

Then he turned over the cards for the Tower, the Fool, the Hermit and the Sun.

"Ah, I see you have had a disaster, indicated by the Tower," he said. "An upheaval, some sort of conflict or catastrophe."

Ravyn nodded her head as tears filled her eyes.

"Here we see the Fool. He is looking off into the distance, about to step off a cliff, with his head in the clouds. He has no plan. He is at risk. You have come to this place with no plan. And you are at risk."

Ravyn felt herself get cold. She reached for her shawl and pulled it around her. "Should I leave?"

"Not necessarily. Let's see what else the cards say. Here we have the Hermit. He holds his lantern up, trying to show the Fool the way. He holds his lantern, to be a guide. You are here to search for answers, are you not, Ravyn? A sign, yes?"

Ravyn nodded again, her tears spilling down her face.

"And here we have the Sun. This is very positive. This card is full of promise and opportunity. Bright things are ahead. Look at the smiling child on the white horse, with sunflowers. This card tells me you will be on a new adventure soon."

"What new adventure?" she asked.

"That is for you to find out," Pablo said. "The Hermit is trying to light your way. And now there is the matter of my fee."

Ravyn's head was swimming with all the information of her tarot reading. She wished she'd written some of it — any of it — down. She reached into her purse, trying to find paper and her wallet.

She found an old receipt and a pen and began scribbling what Pablo had said, looking at the cards. Tower, Fool, risk, Hermit, adventure, and Sun. "How much is the reading?"

"For you, beautiful woman, $20 American," Pablo said, with a smile

Ravyn thought she'd probably been had. Of course, he wanted the fee in American dollars. It probably went farther here. She handed over a $20 bill.

"Thank you, Pablo."

"Ravyn, I must warn you; the cards do say you are at risk. Please be mindful of those around you."

Ravyn rushed into Anica, looking for Sandy. He was waiting by the hostess station, looking a little anxious. Clearly, he was looking for her, too.

"Sorry I'm late. I ran into this tarot reader and he gave me a reading that was interesting, and confusing."

"Oh, did you run into Pablo?"

"Yes, how did you know?"

"He's always preying on our female guests, trying to read 'the cards' to them."

"So, he's not for real?"

Sandy barked out a laugh. "I wouldn't believe anything he says. How much did he charge you?"

"Twenty dollars, American."

"Of course, he did. Listen, I switched with another guy so I have tomorrow completely free. I'm going to take you paddle boarding on the gulf side of Cabo. And I'll have a word with the front desk. Pablo will not bother you again."

Sandy and Ravyn got a table on the covered patio and split an appetizer and ordered a bottle of white wine. Ravyn ordered the fried red snapper while Sandy ordered the pork rib tortellini. When their dinners arrived, they each put a little on each other's plate.

For a split second, it reminded her of Marc. They always did that with their dinners at restaurants.

"Why the sad face?" Sandy asked.

"Oh, just thinking of my fiancé," she said.

"I noticed the ring. And you are here by yourself. So, I guess there's trouble in paradise, as the saying goes."

"Let's just say I'm having my doubts about him. I decided to enjoy a nice time by myself in paradise."

"Well, I'm going to show you a little more of paradise tomorrow. I think you'll like paddle boarding tomorrow morning."

"I will?"

"Yes. When I'm not being a resort waiter, I give standup paddle board lessons and give guided tours. But for you, it's a private lesson and tour tomorrow."

"I've never been paddle boarding."

"Honestly, it's pretty easy. You'll do great."

"Well, that will be fun. Thank you. But are you sure I'm not being a bother? I can stay at the resort in a chaise lounge drinking wine all day."

"Is that what you'd rather do? I figured you for an active girl. Going out and seeing everything there is to do."

"I am an active woman, and I'd rather go paddle boarding."

"OK, meet me in front of the resort at 9 in the morning."

"Nine in the morning? I don't get to sleep in on my vacation?"

"The water will be calm at that time of day and there will be fewer people. If you start later the water will be choppier and there will be more tourists on jet skis. I thought you'd want a better experience."

Ravyn sighed. She did want a better experience; She just wanted to sleep in, too.

"OK, I'll meet you out front at 9," she said. "I had to take a nap this afternoon. This time change is killing me."

"Well, if you give me your room number, I'll make sure I give you a wakeup call," Sandy said.

"No, I'll set my own alarm. And I'll meet you out front tomorrow."

Even though Sandy planted a seed of doubt about Pablo, his warning rang through her mind. "You are at risk. Please be mindful of those around you."

Ravyn woke up just a little before her alarm on Thursday morning. She had washed her bikini the night before, and it wasn't dry, so she pulled out her second bikini. Ravyn was very grateful Julie had suggested she should pack more than one.

It was her cornflower blue bikini with white flowers. She also grabbed her dark navy cover up. She pulled on the same nude sandals she'd worn the day before.

Sandy was waiting out front in his white Jeep. The doors were off and his smile was as white as the vehicle.

"Hey! Are you ready for some fun today?"

"Yes!" Ravyn answered, throwing her canvas bag in the back seat. She pulled herself into the passenger seat and pulled the seatbelt across her torso.

"Hold on!" Sandy said, as he pulled off from the resort's driveway.

Sandy drove way too fast, but Ravyn felt exhilarated. She was laughing and screaming the whole way. She was looking forward to the day of fun ahead.

Marc could hardly sleep Wednesday night. He was anxious to be on his way to Mexico. He'd already texted Ryan Hays, the pilot, twice Thursday morning, asking when they would be able to fly. Ryan's answer was early that afternoon. He'd be off his mandated rest by then.

Marc paced his house, worried what Ravyn was doing. Wondering if she'd believe that he didn't sleep with Laura. He tried texting and calling, but it was no use. She wasn't answering him. Every call now went to voicemail. Her only response to him had been "You bastard."

Was it over? Had he lost her? Marc felt as if he was in a pit of despair. He loved Ravyn. He knew he didn't sleep with Laura. He just needed to convince Ravyn of that and win back her trust.

Ravyn and Sandy got their paddle boards in the water. Sandy was a natural, his lithe, hard body paddling circles around Ravyn.

Ravyn noticed his six-pack abs rising above his board shorts. He really was a good looking guy with a sexy accent. His blond hair and his tanned body seemed to add to his charming nature.

Ravyn tried to keep her balance but ended up in the water a couple of times. She was glad they were staying close to the dock to start. When she finally got the hang of it, Sandy and she paddled out on his tour.

Ravyn wasn't sure how far they'd gone out, but her arms began to ache. "Hey, can we turn around?" she called out.

"Sure! And I have a little surprise back at the dock," Sandy replied.

When they got back to the dock, there was a large white cooler and an insulated bag waiting for them. Inside was a bottle of wine, wine glasses and cheeses, hard salami, crackers, fruit and small sandwiches.

There was even a blanket draped over the cooler. Ravyn spread it out on the nearby beach as Sandy pulled out the wine, popped the cork and placed the food on small plates.

"My gosh! These are real plates! I thought they'd be plastic or paper."

"These are from the resort. We don't do plastic or paper," Sandy admonished.

'This is really nice. Thank you," Ravyn said.

Finished with their picnic and their hunger sated, they went out for another paddle board tour. It was nearing 2 p.m. when they got back to the dock.

Sandy helped Ravyn put the paddle boards away and then they began to walk along the beach. Ravyn carried her sandals in her right hand as Sandy reached for her left hand. She didn't pull away. They walked along in silence, listening to the soothing rush of the waves as they walked in the surf.

Sandy stopped, turned to Ravyn and kissed her. It was a chaste kiss at first, but then he parted her lips and his tongue sought hers. Sandy's mouth began to devour hers, his hands slipping down to her waist and pulling her into him.

Ravyn could feel the erection under his board shorts. Her eyes flew open and she pushed him away.

"No, Sandy. No."

"I didn't see your ring on," he said. "I thought maybe..."

Ravyn looked down at her empty ring finger. "No, I just didn't think it wise to be out on the water with my ring. It's a little loose," she lied.

Sandy wasn't sure he believed Ravyn. Sandy felt a spark when he'd kissed Ravyn. He was sure she was into him.

Sandy reached for Ravyn's hand again and began walking up the beach toward his Jeep. Ravyn suddenly cried out in pain, limping on her right foot.

"What's wrong?" Sandy asked, concerned.

"I stepped on something," Ravyn said, reaching for her foot. She grabbed it, but her hand came away bloody.

"What did you step on?" Sandy asked.

Ravyn saw a piece of broken glass sticking out of her foot. "Ah, ah, ah!" she cried out. "Sandy! Can you pull it out?" Sandy looked at her foot and saw the glass. He held Ravyn's right foot, then gave the glass a firm tug.

Ravyn cried out, and her foot began bleeding profusely.

"I think you might need stitches," Sandy said.

Ravyn's lower lip began to tremble. "Stitches?"

"Yeah, I think so. I was a lifeguard back in Brisbane. I saw a lot of cuts like this. I'd recommend we go to urgent care. Can you walk back to the Jeep or do I need to carry you?"

Ravyn tried not to cry, but her foot hurt so much. She tried to put on her sandal, but it quickly became slick with blood.

"OK, I'll carry you," Sandy said, sweeping Ravyn off her feet and carrying her to his Jeep. Blood dripped off her foot into the sand, a trail of red behind them.

Ravyn tried to keep her right foot out of the Jeep as Sandy drove down the streets of Cabo San Lucas. She was very grateful he knew where he was going.

They pulled up to an urgent care clinic and Sandy picked Ravyn up and carried her inside. Ravyn felt like he was overdoing it by carrying her, but she let him do it anyway. She doubted she could walk on her foot and she certainly didn't want to walk barefoot on the clinic floor. It looked dirty and dingy.

Sandy gently let Ravyn down and explained in rapid Spanish what had happened. Ravyn almost giggled hearing Sandy speak Spanish with an Aussie accent. Then she grew sober. He was really helping her out. She would not have been able to communicate in Spanish with anyone in the clinic.

They sat in the waiting room for about an hour before finally being called back to an exam room. The nurse had called Ravyn's name, but she waved her arm to make sure Sandy came with her.

Ravyn was glad the doctor spoke English.

"Mrs. Shaw, it says you have cut your foot on glass," the doctor said, looking at the paperwork she had first filled out when she and Sandy had arrived at the clinic.

"Yes, sir. On the beach."

"We will get that stitched up. When was the last time you have had a tetanus shot?"

Ravyn tried to think. She remembered getting a tetanus shot when she'd gone for her SCUBA diving lessons. Her instructor had been adamant about her students getting a preventative tetanus shot before the check-out dives in the Florida Keys.

"You don't want to be in a third-world country and need a tetanus shot," her instructor had said.

And here was Ravyn in a foreign country not remembering when her last tetanus shot was.

"I think I might need one," she admitted. "I can't remember when my last one was."

The doctor nodded at the nurse, who disappeared, then returned with a syringe.

Ravyn winced. She wasn't terrified of needles, but she sure didn't enjoy them.

"Which arm do you write with?" the nurse asked in Spanish.

Sandy repeated the question for her in English.

"My right arm," Ravyn replied, pointing to her right arm.

The nurse pinched the flesh on Ravyn's left bicep hard, then jabbed the needle in.

Ravyn cried out.

"This might hurt this afternoon and into tonight," the nurse said. "And you might experience some swelling."

Sandy repeated the nurse's instructions.

Ravyn tried some calming breathing before she replied, "OK."

"I'm going to write you a prescription for some antibiotics, just so you don't end up with an infection," the doctor said. "You're not allergic to any antibiotics, are you?"

"Not that I know of," Ravyn answered truthfully.

"OK," the doctor said, tearing off a paper from his script. "Take the antibiotics twice a day until they are gone. And I've added a prescription for six painkillers at the bottom. You might need those tonight, but just two a day, 12 hours apart, and take them with food."

Sandy walked out of the clinic, with Ravyn limping behind. Ravyn worried about what it had just cost her to receive emergency care. She'd tried to hand over her insurance card, but the administrative clerk had just shaken her head and waved the card away.

Instead, Ravyn had handed over her credit card. The bill was in Mexican pesos. She did a double take when she saw the amount.

There were a lot of zeros in that bill and she had no idea what the exchange rate was.

Sandy helped her into the Jeep, then drove her to a pharmacy where Ravyn stood in a short line to get her painkiller and antibiotic prescriptions filled. Again, she handed over her credit card.

Ravyn's foot was throbbing and her head seemed to pound in time with her foot. Her left arm hurt, too. She realized she'd need those painkillers sooner than she expected.

Marc landed late Thursday afternoon at Cabo San Lucas International Airport, which catered to private planes, and was anxious to disembark.

"Do you know where you are going?" Ryan, the pilot, asked.

"I have the name of the resort where Ravyn is supposed to be," Marc said.

"Well, you have my cell. I'm going to find a nice hotel to get some shut eye and do my pilot's rest. Call me when you're ready to take off, but it will likely have to be Friday afternoon. And I'll have to make the flight plan back to Atlanta, so let me know as soon as you can when we're leaving."

"OK, Ryan. I really appreciate this. I'm getting an Uber or a taxi, really whatever I can get, and head for the resort."

"Do you know where Ravyn is staying? What her room number is?"

"No, I have to check at the front desk. Wish me luck she forgives me quickly," Marc said.

"Bro, I wish you a lot of good karma," Ryan replied.

Chapter 12

Sandy helped Ravyn up to her room, since Ravyn was having trouble putting any weight on her foot.

"Hey, give me your key card," Sandy said.

"Sandy, I can take it from here," she replied, standing in front of her closed door.

"Please, let me help you. I know you're in pain."

"I just want to get in and get into bed. I'm glad I took that pain pill in the car. But I didn't take it with food."

"Why don't we order in. You can get room service. It's included with your package."

"No. I'll go down to one of the restaurants and get some food."

"I'll go with you," Sandy said. "The Lagoon Bar has pizzas."

"OK. I didn't realize how hungry I am. Wait here. I'm just going to put down my purse. I don't need it do I?"

"No, you've got your red band. You're good."

Ravyn opened her door, but Sandy opened the door wider for her and followed her into the suite. He circled his arms around her waist and pulled her to him, kissing her.

Ravyn pushed him away, a little more forcefully than she expected.

"No, Sandy. I asked you to wait outside."

"OK, OK. Can't blame a guy for trying. You are a beautiful woman, Ravyn. I'm very attracted to you," he said, still holding her waist.

"I'm not here for a hookup. I'm here for a little R&R."

"R&R?"

"Rest and relaxation. Now, please wait outside."

Sandy went and stood by the door but didn't exit the room. Ravyn shook her head at him. Don't men ever listen? she wondered. They only ever think with their dicks. Is that what happened with Marc? He was alone with Laura and...?

Ravyn shook her head, trying to rid the thought from her mind. She threw her purse on the side table beside the couch. She really wanted to be left alone tonight, but Sandy was proving he wasn't going to let her.

Ravyn locked the door behind her and stuck her key card in her pocket as she and Sandy walked down the hallway. Well, Ravyn limped rather than walked.

They walked through the lobby and headed outside to Lagoon Bar. Sandy got them a table and pulled the chair out for Ravyn. He pulled another chair over so she could elevate her aching foot.

"That's better," she said.

"Want a glass of wine or a margarita? They are very good here. Maybe a cold beer if you want pizza."

"I'm not sure I should drink anything on this pain pill. The directions were all in Spanish, and my Spanish isn't so good. All I know is I should have taken it with food."

"I'm sure you'll be OK with one drink. What can I get you?"

Ravyn hesitated. Well, her headache had dissipated and her foot wasn't throbbing as badly as it had been. "I guess I'll have a glass of rose."

"Coming right up," Sandy said, moving toward the bar. "Look over the menu," he said over his shoulder.

Ravyn picked up the menu and began to look at the pizzas. The menu had items like pepperoni, margherita, and Hawaiian, but she also saw there were more "exotic" pizzas like the Mexican pizza with chicken, jalapenos and coriander, or the seafood, which had octopus, shrimp and scallops with poblano chile. She wanted to try that one but thought it might be just a bit too spicy for her tonight.

Sandy returned with a Mexican beer for himself and a glass of rose for her. "What did you decide?"

"Hey, you didn't get them to scan my wristband."

"That's OK. I got these. You can get all the food," he said with a wink. "The waiter will be over soon. They are slammed tonight."

"I can see that. I'm thinking about the Mexican pizza. Or do you think that will be too spicy?"

"Do you like spicy food?"

"Yes, but since I took the pain pill, I'm afraid it might be too much for my stomach. Oh wait, they have sushi!"

"You like sushi?"

"I love it. My best friend Julie and I used to go to this sushi place in Buckhead all the time. But the restaurant closed last year."

"Where's Buckhead?"

"Oh, it's a part of Atlanta, and it's called Buckhead. Do you like sushi? Would you split a spicy tuna roll with me?"

"Sure."

"Are the pizzas big? Maybe we should split one."

"We can do that. Maybe we can split a margherita pizza. It's really good and fresh."

"That sounds good, let's do that."

Sandy reached out and grabbed the arm of a passing waiter. "Un momento, I'll be right with you, sir," he said, getting out of Sandy's grip and moving toward another table.

"I may have to go order at the bar," he said.

"Give him a minute," she said, sipping her glass of rose, which was now half empty. She was debating getting another glass. The wine was making her feel relaxed and warm inside.

The waiter returned about 10 minutes later ready to take their order.

Sandy ordered the sushi roll and pizza, then pointed to Ravyn's empty wine glass. "Another?"

"Sure."

"Another rose for the lady and I'll take another one of these," he said, lifting his beer bottle.

"Si, sir," the waiter said, scurrying away.

About 20 minutes later their drinks arrived and another half hour passed before the food arrived. Ravyn was trying to drink more of the water, but her second glass of wine was nearly gone by the time the food arrived.

"We'll take another round," Sandy said, without even asking Ravyn if she wanted more wine. She stuck her wrist out as the waiter scanned her wristband.

"I probably don't need another glass of wine," she said, starting to feel tipsy.

"Well, we don't need anything, but you only live once, right?"

Ravyn smiled. She was going to have to be careful. Maybe Sandy was trying to get her drunk. And now he knew where her room was. She certainly didn't want him to walk her back to her room tonight.

The next round of drinks arrived and their dirty dishes were cleared. The sushi and the pizza had been delicious, Ravyn had to admit.

Now she was feeling more than a little drunk. She probably should not have had the wine with the pain pill. Sandy was starting to swim before her eyes. Oh no, Ravyn thought. I'm in trouble.

Marc's taxi pulled up to the front lobby of the Grand Solmar resort. He quickly paid and nearly ran to the front desk. He impatiently tapped his foot behind the two tourists in front of him.

For what seemed like ages, the pair asked the clerk about the accommodations, then restaurants, then what there was to do at the resort.

My God! Read the website! Marc wanted to shout. The pair finally moved along when the clerk pointed to the bank of elevators.

Marc pressed himself against the desk, saying, "I need the room number for Ravyn Shaw. She might be listed under the room for Rob and Julie Montgomery."

"Are you a guest here, sir?" the clerk asked.

"Does it matter?" Marc asked with exasperation.

The clerk was polite but explained she could not give out room numbers to non-guests.

"You don't understand. My fiancée is here and I should be here with her."

"Is she expecting you? I can ring the room," the clerk said.

"No, she doesn't know I'm here."

"Well, sir, I can't give you the room number. But I can ring her room for you."

The clerk picked up the phone and punched in some numbers but got no answer.

"I'm sorry, sir, there's no answer. Next guest please," the clerk called out to the guest behind Marc.

Frustrated, Marc pushed away from the front desk and began pacing the lobby. Then he noticed a rack of maps and guides of what to do in Cabo. He went over, swiped a map from the rack and snuck into the resort. If the clerk couldn't help him, he'd look for Ravyn himself.

Marc looked at his watch, then the map. Maybe she was at a restaurant.

He went to Anica restaurant first and tried to scan the guests but didn't see anyone who looked like Ravyn. Then he went to Bacari, walking up and down the tables, trying to see if he spotted her. He saw one woman with shoulder-length light brown hair, but when he saw her in profile, he realized it wasn't Ravyn.

Marc began to feel panicked. How was he going to find her? It was like trying to find a needle in a haystack. He was furious the hotel wouldn't give him her room number. He could just go and wait at the door if she wasn't there.

It was getting close to sunset and finding Ravyn would be harder. He picked up his phone and tried calling her. Maybe he'd hear her cell phone ringing. The call immediately went to voicemail. He debated leaving a message but didn't. He'd already left enough of them.

Marc got to the Lagoon Bar and began searching again for Ravyn. As he walked between the tables, he saw a woman who looked like her.

"Ravyn!" he called out.

Ravyn looked up, shocked to see Marc walking toward her.

Marc looked over and saw Sandy sitting across from Ravyn. "Who are you? What are you doing here with my fiancée?"

Sandy stood up and Ravyn attempted to stand up as well, but her stitched foot and all the alcohol she'd had made her very unsteady on her feet. She began to lean away from the table.

Sandy reached out to grab her, trying to keep Ravyn from falling. "Let's get you back to your room, eh, love?"

"Take your hands off her," Marc growled.

"Hey, mate. Not my fault your girlfriend wants to be with me tonight and not you," Sandy shouted back.

"Take your fucking hands off her," Marc said again.

Sandy let go of Ravyn, who abruptly sat down and began to put her head down on the table. She felt sick and Marc and Sandy were shouting at each other.

"Make me," Sandy said, stretching his right arm out and shoving Marc square in his chest.

Without thinking, Marc crouched and took a boxer's stance, pulled back and punched Sandy in the nose, breaking it. Blood began to stream out of Sandy's nose and his eyes watered.

"Motherfucker!" Sandy shouted, taking a swing at Marc, who quickly parried and punched Sandy in his midsection with a quick right, then left.

Sandy gave out an "Oof," and fell back onto a nearby table, plates and glasses shattering when they hit the concrete floor. He held his bloodied nose.

Restaurant patrons began to jump up from their tables. Several men began to crowd around Marc and Sandy, almost cajoling them to fight some more. Phone cameras came out and began to film the scene.

Marc reached down and hauled Ravyn up to her feet. "Where is your room?"

"How did you find me?" she asked, her words slurring. "How did you get here?"

"Julie told me you were here. Where is your room? We need to get out of here."

Ravyn reached in her pocket and pulled out her key card. She tried to take a step with him, but couldn't, limping heavily on her foot.

"What's the matter with you? Are you drunk?"

"My foot. I cut it on some glass on the beach today. I have stitches." Although Ravyn's words came out more like "I how sitches."

"You're drunk," Marc said angrily, as he wrapped Ravyn's left arm over his shoulder and began to walk toward the resort's lobby.

"Ah!" Ravyn cried out. "I got a shot in my arm! That hurts."

Marc pivoted around Ravyn, getting her right arm over his shoulder.

"How much did you have to drink?"

"Three," Ravyn said, holding up three fingers. "I don't think I was supposed to drink with the pain pills."

"Pain pills? You drank with pain pills?"

"My foot really hurt! And my head. Now I don't feel so good."

Marc got up to Ravyn's room and unlocked it, steering her inside. "Are you going to be sick?"

"I'm not sure. Maybe."

Marc got her into the bathroom just in time for Ravyn to be sick in the toilet. He got a washcloth and poured cold water over it before wiping up Ravyn's face. He rinsed it out and held the cold compress to her forehead.

Ravyn slumped over the toilet, passing out.

"OK, Ravyn, let's get you in bed. You're going to have to sleep this off."

Ravyn was dead weight as Marc laid her down on the bed. He removed her sandals but couldn't get any more clothes off of her. He could see the bandage on her right foot.

Marc reached for a glass and hoped there was scotch in the minibar. He was glad to see there was. He poured himself a glass before calling Ryan, letting him know they'd be leaving the next day.

"You found her then?" Ryan asked.

"I did. But she's passed out on the bed now. Cut her foot, took some pain pills and downed them with alcohol. She's not going anywhere tonight."

"Oh, that's not good."

"No, it's not. But we'll leave tomorrow, OK?"

"But she's alright? She's breathing?"

"She's breathing. I can hear her snoring. She gets like that when she's really out."

"OK. I'll make the flight plans in the morning," Ryan said.

Marc had the phone to his ear and was about to pour himself a second scotch when there was a sudden sharp knock at the door and the key card lock disengaged. Two security officers and another serious looking man entered the room.

"Hey, some men are breaking into my room!" Marc said, dropping his glass.

"What?" Ryan asked. "Marc? Marc?"

Marc's cell phone fell to the floor as the security officers tackled him to the ground, putting handcuffs on him.

Chapter 13

Ravyn awoke Friday morning unsure how she'd gotten into her room. Had Sandy brought her there?

She felt a wave of relief that her clothes were still on. She had an awful taste in her mouth. She vaguely thought she might have been sick.

Ravyn sat up, her head swimming. She looked around and saw a cell phone on the floor.

It looked like Marc's phone. But why would it be in her room? Was Marc here? She picked up the phone and saw it was out of power. She plugged it into her charger.

"Marc?" she called out hesitantly.

She reached for her phone and found one message from a number she didn't recognize. It seemed like it might be a local call. This time, she listened to the voice message.

"Ravyn, it's Marc. I'm at the police station in Cabo. I've been arrested. I need your help. Here's the address, and I need you to call Ryan Hays, our pilot. I'm not sure if they'll let me out of custody today. Call Ryan and tell him that. Here is his number."

Marc gave the number so fast, Ravyn had to listen to the number twice.

Marc? In custody? Ravyn was suddenly very frightened. Why was Marc at the police station?

She had hazy memories of Marc and Sandy in a fight, of being helped to her room. Her right foot hurt and she remembered cutting it. Had Marc helped her into her room? It must have been. Where was Sandy?

Ravyn started the write the number down but found the number for Ryan in Marc's phone and dialed it.

"Hello?"

"Is this Ryan?"

"Speaking. Who's this?"

"This is Ravyn. Marc's at the police station in Cabo. I don't know what to do!"

"Wait, what? Slow down. Marc's in jail? I thought he'd found you last night."

"He did, but I don't remember much. I took these pain pills for my foot and I guess I shouldn't have had any alcohol. I don't really remember what happened."

"I was on the phone with him last night, but we got cut off. He said some people broke into the room and then we got cut off. Where are you?"

"I'm still at the resort. He gave me the address for the police station. I'm going to go there now. But he said we might not be able to fly out today. Are you flying us out?"

"I am. Or I thought I was. Listen, are you OK? Are you hurt?"

"My foot is throbbing. But I'd better not take another pain pill. I'll just take some ibuprofen or something. Oh, the doctor gave me some antibiotics so my foot doesn't get infected. I think I forgot to take one last night."

"You go to the police station and see if you can get Marc out on bail, or whatever. I'll see what I can do about flight plans for tomorrow."

"OK," Ravyn said, but her voice was cracking.

Ravyn quickly showered, gasping as the hot water found her stitched foot. Her dressing was now wet, but she didn't have another bandage. She only had small bandages in her purse. Ones used to cover a small cut. But she'd have to use those. She had no choice. She wished she'd thought to buy bigger bandages when she was at the pharmacy getting her prescriptions.

She got dressed and pulled her damp hair back in a ponytail. She hesitated as she saw her engagement ring on the bedside table. She put it on reluctantly. As she slipped it on her finger, she began to cry.

Ravyn limped in circles in her room, gulping air, trying to calm herself down. She got a glass of water and drank that, before remembering she needed to take her antibiotics, too. She swallowed the bitter pill.

Ravyn wiped her eyes and blew her nose before heading down to the lobby. She ran into Sandy near the front door.

Her eyes grew wide when she saw his face. He had two black eyes and a brace on his nose.

"What happened to you?" she asked with alarm.

"Your fucking boyfriend happened to me, that's what. I'll press charges! He broke my nose."

Only it all came out muffled when Sandy said it. She could see he had cotton up his nose, too.

"What are you doing at work? Shouldn't you be home, resting?"

"Listen, bitch, I took a day off to be with you. A lot of good that did me! You and your boyfriend need to leave me alone."

Ravyn was taken aback. Had Marc broken Sandy's nose? As if through a haze she remembered Marc finding her and getting angry with Sandy. Did Sandy take a swing at Marc first? She thought maybe he had.

"Well, you started it," she said to Sandy's back.

Sandy just turned to her and sneered. "Get out, bitch!"

Ravyn saw a taxi pulling up to disgorge tourists and tried to step in as soon as they left.

"Miss, you can't be in here," the taxi driver said.

"I need you to take me to this address," she said, giving him the address for the police station and getting into the taxi. "I'll pay cash. American dollars. Just drive."

"American dollars?" The driver shrugged and pulled away from the resort.

Ravyn's taxi pulled in front of a drab brown building. "You want this address, miss? Estación de policía. The police, si?"

"Yes. I don't know how long I'll be so don't wait for me," she said, handing over the last of her dollars. Ravyn would have to find an ATM to get more cash.

The taxi driver drove off and Ravyn limped up the concrete steps. Every step sent a wave of pain through her foot.

For the second time in her life, Ravyn found herself in a foreign police station and afraid.

She approached a woman she assumed was an administrative clerk and prayed the woman spoke English.

"Hello, do you speak English? I'm here to speak with a man in custody. Marc Linder?" Ravyn said his name as a question. She tried again. "I'm here to see Marc Linder." Then she spelled out his name.

The woman held up a finger, stood up and walked around her desk, saying, "Un momento." The woman disappeared down the hall, returning with a short dark-haired man with cold black eyes.

"You are here to see the man, Marc Linder?" the man said.

"Yes."

"Are you his abogada?" he asked.

Ravyn stared blankly. She had no idea what he was asking.

"His attorney. Are you his attorney?"

"No, I'm his fiancée."

"He's not having visitors today," the man said, firmly.

"Why is he here? Has he been arrested? I'll get an attorney."

"He is charged with public disturbance and property damage."

"Well, can I bail him out of here? There's bail for that, yes?"

"No bail. He has to go before the magistrado, the magistrate."

"I want to see him, now," Ravyn said with more courage than she had. "And I will sit in this lobby until I get to see him."

Ravyn could see the woman look at Ravyn and then back to the sour man.

"Can't you see she's worried about her man? You should let her see her fiancé. You can see she has a pretty engagement ring on."

The dark-haired man looked over to Ravyn and spied the diamond on her hand.

"Well, maybe just this once," he said. "I will make an exception for you."

The man walked Ravyn back into the police station, stopping before a locked door. The officer took from his pocket a large ring of keys, picked one and opened the door.

Ravyn could see Marc sitting on a bench but screamed when he looked up at her. His face was bruised and he had a cut on his cheek.

"Marc!" she said, rushing to him. She grabbed him in a hug, but Marc gasped in pain.

"That hurts," he said in barely a whisper.

"What hurts? What happened?" Ravyn turned to face the officer. "What did you do to him?" she demanded.

"He fell. It was an accident."

"An accident my ass! I want a lawyer and I want one now."

"Ah, miss, you aren't in America."

A cold chill ran through Ravyn. It was like she was back in the police station in Rome. A foreigner in a foreign police station.

"What's his bail?"

"There is no bail. He needs to go before the magistrate. You have to come back tomorrow."

"No, we're leaving now," she said.

"I'm afraid that's not possible."

"What do you want? Money? Is that what you want to release him?"

"Miss, that would be a bribe. I don't accept bribes."

"What if I give you this ring?" Ravyn said, taking her engagement ring off.

"That would be a bribe, and I told you I can't accept a bribe. But," he said slowly, "if you were to leave the ring behind, it would be lost and how could I return it to you? I can't."

"Ravyn, no," Marc pleaded. "Please, no. That's your engagement ring."

"I want his passport and wallet," Ravyn said.

The officer left the room, returning with Marc's passport and an empty wallet. The cash and credit cards were gone.

"Why is this empty?" Ravyn demanded.

"It was empty before he got here," the officer said. "He must have been robbed."

Ravyn showed the ring to the dark-haired officer and placed it on the bench next to Marc. She then helped Marc up.

"Please, Ravyn. Don't do this. This ring symbolizes our love. I'll get out of here, eventually."

Ravyn felt as if her heart might break, seeing Marc hurt. "Marc, my love isn't represented by a piece of jewelry. Now let's get out of here while we can."

Chapter 14

Marc and Ravyn took a taxi back to the resort, Ravyn gingerly helping Marc into and out of the car. Every bounce in the road on the ride made Marc wince.

"I guess it's too late today to fly out," Marc said as they got back to her room.

"Your phone is there," Ravyn said, pointing. "It's charged. Why don't you call Ryan and find out."

"Oh, you have it. I couldn't find it after I was arrested. I thought the police kept it."

Ravyn got a glass of water and handed Marc one of her pain pills. "You look like you need this more than I do. I have four left, and you can take another one tonight. The doctor said I could take two a day. You'll have some for the flight home."

Marc hesitated, but then took the pill from her outstretched hand, gulping it down with the water.

"Are you hungry? I can order room service."

"Yes, I'm starved. I haven't eaten since yesterday."

"Looks like they've got steaks. Do you want a steak?"

"No. A sandwich, maybe two, will be great."

Ravyn ordered a chicken sandwich, two club sandwiches, a small salad, a sushi roll, then ordered a bottle of Chardonnay. "It's not for you," she said as Marc gave her a look.

"If I'm going to lose my engagement ring today, I'm going to drink heavily this afternoon."

"I wish you hadn't done that," Marc said. "I mean it's insured, but I'm not sure I could make a claim if you willingly left it at the police station."

"What are you talking about? I was out paddle boarding yesterday, and it fell off in the water. I told you it was loose."

"Ravyn, you are not about to commit insurance fraud."

Marc shuffled into the bathroom to assess the damage to his face. "Doesn't look too bad," he said, looking at the cut on his cheek. "I don't think there will be a scar."

He came back to the couch and sat next to Ravyn, who curled up next to Marc as they awaited their food.

"Can you tell me what happened?" she asked, pointing to his bruised face.

"Let's just say I now know how the punching bag at the gym feels."

"What do you mean? They assaulted you?"

"I gather they would say I was 'uncooperative.' My whole body hurts. I'm afraid to take my shirt off. I think they might have rearranged some internal organs."

Ravyn began to lift his light green polo shirt. "Oh my God! Marc, we need to get you to a hospital! You are all bruised."

"Let's see if we can get some ice on that."

Ravyn went to the bathroom and grabbed a towel, then put as many ice cubes as the tiny fridge in the hotel room had.

"This might not help much," she said, placing the towel under his shirt. "I'll have to find out where the ice maker is on the floor."

Marc winced again from the cold, but after a while he thought it was helping.

The food arrived and the waiter set the tray down on the small table. Another waiter placed the wine bucket on the table before opening the Chardonnay. Ravyn stuck out her wristband for the scan.

"Good thing Rob and Julie got the all-inclusive plan. I'm out of cash and you are, too," Ravyn said. "I still have my credit cards, but I might be close to my maximum. I don't know how much I spent at the clinic getting my foot stitched. And I charged my flight here on the card, too."

"I'll have to cancel my cards when we get home. Not sure how much good it will do. They've probably charged hundreds, if not thousands, on those cards."

"Your bank won't flag the charges? Especially if they are being made in Cabo?"

"Maybe."

"I think we should order in for dinner tonight, too, and breakfast tomorrow. You don't need to be moving around. And you don't need to run into Sandy, either. You broke his nose."

"Sandy? Is that the guy you were with?"

"Yes, he is a waiter here. He was just trying to be friendly."

"I bet. Just how friendly was he?"

"Marc, nothing happened with me and Sandy."

"Just like nothing happened between me and Laura," Marc said, raising his voice. "I wondered when we'd get around to this conversation."

"A conversation about how you slept with Laura? Sure, let's have that conversation," Ravyn said, angry.

"I did not sleep with her. And instead of answering any of my calls or texts, you take off for Mexico! You ran away!"

"What was I supposed to do?" Ravyn shrieked, jumping up from the couch.

"Talk to me, Ravyn!"

"But there's that photo," Ravyn said through gritted teeth. "Have you seen it? How do you explain that?"

"I've seen it, Ravyn. Julie sent it to me," Marc shot back. "And I don't know how to explain it. I think she took it the night before I left. She came up to my room with wine. Uninvited, I might add.

She was trying to seduce me, I admit that, but I asked her to leave and she did. I can't figure out how she got back in my room."

"Did you lock your room? Or did you leave the door unlocked for her?"

"I did not leave my door unlocked for her! It was locked!" Marc shouted. "Maybe she left it unlocked when she left. Maybe that's what happened."

"But she's on your bed with her boob hanging out! It sure looks like you slept with her!"

"I did not sleep with her! I could never, ever do that to you. I love you too much."

"I want to believe you," Ravyn said, beginning to cry.

Marc eased himself off the couch and went over to Ravyn to hug her. She pulled away at first, then hugged him back.

"Hey, careful. Don't squeeze so hard."

"I love you, too. I'm sorry I came here," Ravyn said. "I'm sorry. I just needed to get away and think."

"About what?"

"About us, whether I could trust you."

"Goddammit, Ravyn! Nothing happened. Please say you believe me, or there might not be an us."

Marc could see Ravyn's doubt in her face, but then she whispered, "I believe you."

Marc began to cry, relief washing over him. Ravyn had never seen Marc cry. Suddenly she was weeping, too. They clung to each other.

Marc and Ravyn left their uneaten lunch on the table, moving over to the bed.

"I'm not sure I can," Marc started to say, but Ravyn put a finger to his lips.

"Let's just lie here for a while. Be still."

"I don't have a change of clothes. Can you get my pants off?"

She began to undo his belt and pulled his cargo pants down, realizing she'd need to get his socks and shoes off first. She got his pants off, leaving his boxers on.

"I think I'll have to leave my shirt on," Marc said. "I'm not sure I can raise my arms."

"Oh, Marc," she said, starting to cry again.

"Don't cry, don't cry," he said, bending his elbow so he could stroke her face without raising his arm.

Ravyn curled up next to Marc, feeling the warmth of his body. "I can feel your heartbeat," she said.

"It will only ever beat for you. I love you."

"I love you, too," she said, listening to his slow, steady breath as they both fell asleep.

They awoke hours later to darkness. Marc tried to roll over and groaned, then took a sharp intake of breath.

"Are you still in pain?" Ravyn asked.

Marc just shook his head. "I'm not really sure how mobile I'm going to be tomorrow for the flight. My whole torso hurts. I dread climbing the stairs. Do you have another pain pill?"

"I do. I'll get it."

"Thanks. That leaves two for tomorrow?"

"Three."

"Is there any liquor in the minibar?"

"Yes, but I can also order up cocktails. You want a scotch?"

"See if they have Macallan 12-year or Glenlivet 12-year. Have them send two doubles."

"Do you want some fresh food? We never even ate our lunch. We could order dinner. I still have the bottle of wine. I barely touched it."

"Let's order fresh food, although I'm not that hungry. I just hurt too much."

"You're supposed to take the pain pill with food, That's what the doctor said. And we never ate. We could microwave the sandwiches, I guess. Let me help you to the chair. I'll order some appetizers and your scotch."

"See if you can buy a bottle of either brand, since this is all inclusive. I might need the bottle," Marc said, wincing as he tried to sit up on the bed. He swung his legs over and tried to breathe deeply. "Help me get my pants back on. I can't reach down. I may have some bruised ribs. I've really stiffened up."

Ravyn hobbled over to Marc, helped him get dressed, then helped him to stand and guided him to the cushioned chair. He sat down with a whoosh of air. "I may have to sleep in this chair tonight. Not sure I can get up again."

"I'll help you," she said, quickly getting dressed as well.

"I really don't think you can. I really may be in this chair for the night."

"I'll order the food and drinks. We'll see after that."

Ravyn was not exactly surprised when the resort staff said they couldn't send up an entire bottle of scotch, so she ordered three doubles and hoped it would help ease Marc's pain.

"I better call Ryan before I get wasted tonight. I need to find out when we're leaving tomorrow."

She poured a glass of the Chardonnay and realized there was no ice left in the tiny fridge's freezer to make it cold. She couldn't drink warm white wine. She'd have to go hunt for the ice maker. They'd probably need a bucket for tonight to help with Marc's pain anyway.

"You call him while I go find some ice."

Ravyn put on her left sandal, but had trouble getting her right one on. She decided she'd go down the hall barefoot. She'd seen some tourists walk down the hall that way.

She returned with a full ice bucket and remembered she'd neglected to take her antibiotics that day. She was supposed to take two a day, right? Was that what the doctor said? Ravyn couldn't remember so she just took one pill. She'd have to remember to take another tomorrow and she'd just finish them off when she got back to Atlanta.

Atlanta. Home. She couldn't wait to leave Mexico. *I was so in a hurry to get here, and now I'm in a hurry to leave,* she thought.

Cabo San Lucas, like her trip to Rome, was going to hold bittersweet memories.

The knock at the door meant the food had arrived, along with Marc's drinks. Ravyn brought the first one to him and he gulped it down in two swallows.

"I think we're going to need a few more of these," she told the server.

"Very good, madam," he replied, turning to leave the room. "How many?"

Marc held up three fingers.

Marc and Ravyn proceeded to get a little drunk that night; Marc more so than Ravyn. When she finished the bottle, she put it in the trash and didn't order anything else.

"It's getting late," Ravyn said. "What time should I set my alarm?"

"Ryan says we can't fly out until 3 o'clock tomorrow afternoon."

"We'll get home late then."

"He said it was about a 4 ½ hour flight, maybe less."

"I thought it was longer coming out here," Ravyn responded.

"Maybe it was, but we're not flying commercial."

"Well, then I won't set my alarm. We'll just get up when we get up. We can have breakfast and lunch before we go. I should probably order to-go sandwiches for Ryan and the co-pilot, yes? There is a co-pilot, right?"

"Yes. I'm sure they would appreciate it."

"Might as well get all we can out of the all-inclusive, especially since we're leaving a day early."

"You want to stay another day?" Marc asked.

"Absolutely not."

"I didn't think so, but I thought I'd ask."

"Let me help you out of that chair and into bed."

"Ravyn, I don't think you can."

"You will really stiffen up in that chair and then we'll never get you out. Come on, give me your arm and I'll try to leverage you out."

Marc gave her his arm, but he ended up pulling Ravyn over, nearly on top of him.

"Told you."

"You did that on purpose. Now be serious. Let me help you up."

"Forget it."

"I'll give you a blow job if you let me help you out of the chair."

Marc smiled a drunken smile. "Well, now you're talking."

Ravyn called down to the front desk Saturday morning and said she would be checking out early and asked to have a taxi take them back to the Cabo San Lucas International Airport. Ravyn held two sandwiches in a bag for Ryan and the co-pilot, plus two more for their dinner that night on the plane.

Ryan was walking around the plane doing his pre-flight checks when Marc and Ravyn walked up.

"What the hell happened to you?" Ryan asked, seeing Marc's face and watching him walk like an old man.

"I had an unfortunate meeting with the Mexican police," Marc said.

"With your face?"

"Yeah, and the rest of me. Do you have scotch on board?"

"Yeah man, help yourself. We should be airborne in about an hour."

Ravyn handed over the bag with the sandwiches. "I hope you like chicken," she said.

"I'm vegan," Ryan deadpanned, watching Ravyn's face as it fell. "No, I'm kidding. Thanks. You must be Ravyn," he said, taking her bag with his left hand and extending his right hand to shake hers.

"I am."

"I can see why Marc wanted to find you."

Ravyn blushed. "I hope he won't regret it."

"He won't," Marc interrupted. "Ryan, can you give me a hand up the stairs. I think my ribs are bruised. I'm not really sure I will make it up."

"Sure, sure. Give me your arm."

Ryan took Marc's arm, then stood behind him as Marc walked up each step, taking a break at each one, before he got into the cabin of the jet. Ravyn limped her way up the stairs and settled into a lounge chair opposite Marc.

"You two make yourselves comfortable. There are some snacks in that drawer, and there's bottled water, wine, some liquor over there."

"Any ice?" Ravyn asked. "I've been icing down Marc's bruises."

"Dude, they really did a number on you," Ryan said, shaking his head. "Ice is over in that container."

Marc just closed his eyes and shook his head in the affirmative. He felt relaxed now that he knew they were headed home.

"Right, I'll make an announcement when we're ready to take off."

After a half hour, Ryan came on the intercom and announced they would be delayed and should get clearance for takeoff sometime after 4 p.m. "Sorry about that," he said. "There's some weather ahead and we're hoping to let it settle."

"How old is Ryan?" Ravyn asked, noticing how young he looked. "Is he old enough to fly this plane?"

"That was my thought when I met him. I assure you he can fly this plane."

Finally, the engines roared to life and they stood on the tarmac waiting for takeoff. Marc and Ravyn heard the high whine of the engines as they headed down the runway. Ryan's liftoff was perfect and they were airborne.

"Fix me another drink, will you, Ravyn?" Marc said, extending his hand with his empty glass. "And do you have another pain pill?"

"Do you want another drink, or something else to ease the pain?" Ravyn asked.

"Something else?"

"Do they have video cameras back here? You know, to watch us?"

"I don't think so. Why?"

"I was just thinking. I'll never get another chance to…"

"To what?"

"To have sex on a private jet," she whispered.

"I don't think you have to whisper. But I'm not sure this is a good idea. I can barely move."

Ravyn stood up and grabbed a blanket. "What if I help you over to the couch?"

"Well, you dirty girl. You really want to join the mile-high club."

Ravyn smiled a little wicked grin. "I do."

Marc managed to maneuver slowly over to the couch and Ravyn undid his pants. She slipped out of her shorts and covered her lower half with the blanket. "Just in case anyone can see us."

"I really don't think they can."

"Just in case," she said, as she began to give Marc a hand job, getting him erect.

"That would work a whole lot better with your tongue," he said.

Ravyn smiled again before she began to go down on him, circling the tip of his penis with her tongue before sucking it. Marc closed his eyes and groaned, then smiled. He was going to join the mile-high club with Ravyn. Laura Lucas had been completely wrong on that count.

Ravyn eventually lowered herself on Marc's erection, as Marc rubbed her clit. They climaxed at almost the same time.

Marc and Ravyn slept after their lovemaking, curled up awkwardly on the small couch, awaking about an hour before they were to land back at PDK. Ravyn pulled out their sandwiches and pulled two bottled waters out of an ice chest on board.

"Oh, hell. My car is at Hartsfield," Ravyn said, as they were about to land. "How will we get home?"

"My car's at PDK, Ravyn. I'll drive us home and we'll get your car tomorrow."

"Oh right. I think we should stop at urgent care to see about your injuries. What if your ribs are broken?"

"Ravyn, right now I want to go home and sleep in my own bed."

"But what if…"

"If it's bad tomorrow we can go to urgent care."

After they landed, Ryan helped Marc down the stairs and Ravyn helped him into the passenger's seat of his car. Her foot hurt when she pressed on the gas but she tried not to let Marc see.

She took steady breaths as she accelerated after each red light on Buford Highway and she seemed to be hitting every one of them. Eventually she turned on Lindbergh and then into their neighborhood. Ravyn could have wept when she saw the front door to their house.

Marc had fallen asleep in the car. He'd taken that pain pill and downed it with another scotch.

"Hey, honey," she said, shaking his arm. "We're home."

"What?" he said, his eyes unfocused as he roused himself.

"We're home. Let me come around and help you out of the car."

Ravyn opened the passenger door, while Marc swung his legs to plant them on the ground. He winced with every move. "I think I can get it," he said, his arms pushing him upright, but pushed with a little too much force and almost fell into Ravyn. She was glad she was there to stop him from falling.

"Guess I shouldn't have taken that pain pill with alcohol, huh?"

"You should have learned from my mistake. Let's get you up the steps and into bed."

"That sounds wonderful. You're wonderful, you know that?" he said with a slight slur.

"I think that's the pain pill and alcohol talking."

"No, it's not," Marc said, stopping in the living room. "I thought I'd lost you, again, Ravyn. Thanks to Laura."

Ravyn could see tears in his eyes and she could feel her eyes welling, too. "I thought I'd lost you to Laura Lucas, Marc."

"You'll never lose me to her. Never, never. It's you I want. It's you I love. I want a life with you. I want a family with you, Ravyn. No one else."

Chapter 15

Marc and Ravyn slept late Sunday morning. Marc took another pain pill from Ravyn's stash and then found some old painkillers from some dental surgery he had years ago. He'd never tossed the remainder of the pills out and he was grateful now, although he wasn't so sure how potent they'd be. Just as long as he could keep the pain in his ribs down. It hurt to take a deep breath. It hurt to roll over in bed. It hurt to do anything.

Ravyn and Marc made love, then fell back asleep. They were exhausted from the Mexican trip, the flight home and the emotional upheaval they'd both endured.

By Sunday afternoon, both had showered and dressed.

"Want to go pick up your car?" Marc asked.

"Can you drive? Why don't you drop me off at the Lindbergh MARTA station and I'll take the train down to the airport and drive my car back?"

"Are you sure?"

"Yeah, I'm sure."

"OK. I've got to call all my credit card companies, too. Jesus I'm glad I have that list in the fire box."

Marc gingerly got into his car and drove Ravyn to the train station. He was grateful he didn't have to drive all the way down to Hartsfield-Jackson Atlanta International Airport and back home.

His ribs still ached and his skin on his torso was purple from the bruising. His face was less so. It seemed to be healing quickly. He got home and began making calls to the eight credit card companies, canceling the accounts, finding out which ones had been used, and ordering all new cards.

When he was finished, he decided to try shaving, but he did so gently.

Ravyn arrived back home nearly two hours later.

"I was beginning to worry about you," Marc said.

"There was some problem on the lines and we were stopped on the tracks for about 20 minutes. I didn't have a cell signal to call you. By the time I got to the car, I was just ready to come home."

"Well, I'm glad you're home. Are you hungry? We could order a pizza. I don't have anything thawed out to cook."

"That sounds great. Mushroom and olives pizza or pepperoni?"

"How about half and half?"

"Perfect."

"What are we going to do about your engagement ring?" Marc asked.

"Why don't I just wear my little sapphire and diamond ring on my left hand until we know how long it will take."

"But that's not an engagement ring."

"It can be if I want it to be."

"If we can't make a claim on insurance, I'll go to Tiffany's and get you another one. This time you come with me and pick it out."

"If we can't make the insurance claim, I'll just keep wearing this one," she said, having put her favorite ring on her left hand.

"But that won't match the wedding band I planned to pick out."

"You picked out a band, too?"

159

"It's sapphires and diamonds. It's very pretty. Mine is just a plain band."

"No fancy ring for you?"

"No fancy ring for me. Julie made it very clear *you* were to get the fancy ring."

"Well, we can pick out our bands together. Maybe there's a fancy ring you will like."

Marc smiled. "I'd be fine wearing a piece of tinfoil on my finger if it meant I was married to you."

The pizza arrived and Ravyn took her antibiotic and Marc took the last of Ravyn's pain pills. They each had a glass of wine. Two hours later as the sun was setting, they turned in for the night.

"I must be feeling better," Marc said.

"Why's that?"

"I'm feeling a little frisky tonight. I keep remembering the flight home."

"Do you think Ryan knew what we were doing?"

"If he did, I suppose he's too much of a professional to say he knows what goes on in the cabin. I'm sure we've not been the first couple to make love on that plane."

"I hope they disinfect the plane after each trip. I don't really want to think about the people who have done it on that couch."

"We've done it on that couch," Marc said, wiggling his eyebrows.

"Not that I think I'll ever fly on that plane again, but I don't know if I can look at that couch again without blushing."

Marc carefully rolled over to hold Ravyn. "I liked what we did on that plane. Want to do it again?"

Even in the growing duskiness in the bedroom, Marc could see Ravyn smile.

Ravyn called Julie a few days after Memorial Day in hopes they could have lunch so she could tell her what had happened in Cabo

San Lucas. She'd texted when she'd landed back in Atlanta to let her know she was OK but hadn't told her the whole story.

"Hey, this week is a little crazy," Julie said. "The girls are starting tennis camp, but how about we have lunch next week at Seven Lamps? Oh, and I got good news about my cysts. Both benign."

"Julie, that is wonderful news. I'd love to celebrate your good news at Seven Lamps. I love that place. The waffle fries are awesome."

"OK, let's meet up next weekend."

But by Friday, Julie texted that she couldn't make their lunch date. She asked if they could reschedule for the following Saturday, so it was a little more than two weeks after Ravyn returned from Mexico before she saw Julie.

Ravyn was sitting at an outside table on the patio by the restaurant when Julie walked up.

"Sorry I'm late," she said, throwing her hot pink Louis Vuitton handbag on the table.

"I'm glad you could make it. I thought I might have to postpone again. I haven't been feeling well this week."

"What's up?"

"I think it's just the stress of what happened. I'm feeling better this afternoon and I'm really hungry."

"Well, I want to hear all about the trip. Was the resort nice?"

"Oh, it was. And Marc and I were really glad you had the all-inclusive package when his cash and credit cards were stolen by the police. We were able to order room service."

"Wait a minute, Marc's money was stolen by the police?" Julie asked, puzzled. Then she squinted her eyes at Ravyn, noticing her left hand. "And where's your engagement ring?"

"Marc got arrested after he punched Sandy. And the ring is back at the police station in Cabo. That was essentially Marc's bail money."

"What? Who's Sandy? Is that a guy or girl?"

"A guy. I met him the first day I got there."

"Maybe you need to start at the beginning."

Ravyn recounted how she'd met Sandy the first day, how he'd taught her to paddle board the next day, how she'd cut her foot and had to go to the clinic. She recounted the pain pills and the wine she'd drunk. How Marc had found her in the bar with Sandy and punched him.

She also described her going to the police station after Marc was detained and how she'd had to leave her ring behind to get him out of custody.

Ravyn told her Marc had been roughed up by the police and she was glad she hadn't taken all of the pain pills the clinic had prescribed. Marc had needed them.

Julie stared at Ravyn wild eyed. This was the stuff of a James Bond novel.

"Is Marc OK?"

"He is now. The bruising is mostly gone. It's kind of a greenish yellow now on his chest."

"And, how are you?"

"Oh, I'm fine. I finished off all the antibiotics. No infection."

"What?"

"I cut my foot on a piece of glass on the beach. That's why I had to go to the clinic. I needed stitches. That's why I had the pain pills for Marc."

"That sounds like more excitement than I'd want to have."

"Oh, I didn't tell you the best part," Ravyn said, leaning over the table. "Marc and I did it on the private plane."

"You did? You joined the mile-high club?"

"We did. It was kind of thrilling."

"Did you and Marc use condoms?"

"No. I'm on the pill remember? We haven't used those for months."

"Ravyn, you know some antibiotics can make the pill less effective. When was your last period?"

"Ahh, I had it last week, but it was really light. I think it was just the stress of the trip, though."

"Then you're probably OK, but you might want to take a pregnancy test just to be sure."

"Julie, I'm not pregnant."

"When you said you weren't feeling well, what did you mean?"

"I've just felt off. I've felt really queasy in the mornings when I first get up, but I feel fine in the afternoons."

"Ravyn, you are describing what sounds a lot like morning sickness. I should know. I had it awful with both girls in the beginning of my pregnancies."

"Julie, I am not pregnant."

"Well go online and see if those antibiotics make the pill ineffective."

"I threw the bottle out when I finished them. And the instructions were all in Spanish anyway, so I couldn't read them. I will say this, healthcare in Mexico is cheap. I finally got my credit card bill for the clinic. I was expecting several hundred dollars, but it wasn't that bad."

"Great. If you don't have the pill bottle, you better take a pregnancy test. And no more wine until you find out if you are pregnant," Julie said, reaching over the table, grabbing Ravyn's half glass of white wine and downing it with one gulp.

"Hey!" Ravyn exclaimed. "You owe me another glass of wine!"

"No, ma'am, not until you take the test and you know for sure."

"Julie, you are being ridiculous."

"No, I'm not. Take the test."

Ravyn left Seven Lamps feeling unsettled. She couldn't be pregnant. She didn't feel pregnant, not that she'd know how a pregnant woman would feel.

She'd just been a little queasy. Probably picked up some kind of Mexican bug. She was glad she didn't return with any sort of horrible digestive distress. Well, I'm not going to worry about it, because I'm not pregnant, she told herself. I had my period. Julie's just being a mother hen.

Ravyn was busy training for the upcoming Peachtree Road Race 10K on July 4. She enjoyed running in Marc's Garden Hills neighborhood. Some of the streets were tree lined, keeping her in the shade during her hot summer runs.

Ravyn mapped out a 3-mile route and ran it twice to get miles in. The neighborhood had just enough hills to make her feel like she was ready for Cardiac Hill and the other hills along the Peachtree Road Race route.

As she got closer to July Fourth, she found herself getting a bit winded on her second loop. She thought that was odd but thought maybe she was overtraining. She was grateful she would taper in two days, running just one loop to save her legs for the race.

Ravyn was excited she'd gotten a good number for the Peachtree Road Race, starting close to the front of the pack.

Ever since her lunch with Julie, Ravyn had been declining wine with dinner. "I need to keep hydrated. I need water," she said.

Marc had looked at her puzzled, but she just told him she was training for the Peachtree and didn't want any wine until after the race.

In fact, Ravyn was debating whether she should take a pregnancy test. It would put her mind at ease, she thought. But every time she went to the grocery store, she couldn't bring herself to buy one.

The morning of July 4, Ravyn got up early, feeling queasy. It's nerves, she thought. She ate some toast with peanut butter, drank some orange juice and scrambled one egg.

Then Ravyn woke Marc up so he could drive her to the Lindbergh MARTA station. He'd offered to drive her up to the start of the race at Lenox Square, but she said she could take MARTA and feel the excitement of the race start.

It would be strange this year to finish the race in Piedmont Park and not be able to just walk home to her old condo in Midtown. She'd have to return to the Lindbergh station via the Midtown MARTA station and call Marc to pick her up.

Ravyn finished a little slower than she expected, but still ran a decent race. She met up with several Atlanta Track Club friends before heading to the Midtown MARTA station. She called Marc to tell him she was on the way to Lindbergh, then called him again when she arrived.

"I'm right outside the gate," Marc said. "MARTA security has chased me off once already."

Ravyn walked out of the gate and stood at the curb before she saw Marc's BMW. She waved and turned off her phone, getting into his car.

"How was the race?" he asked.

"It was good, but I felt a little winded toward the end. I was ready for a big push toward the finish and I didn't have anything in the tank."

"Well, let's get you home, then we can go out to celebrate," Marc said.

"Sounds good."

Marc and Ravyn ended up at Fellini's Pizza near their house and ordered a pizza and a pitcher of beer.

Marc poured Ravyn a pint, then one for himself. Ravyn tried to sip at her beer but ended up drinking two glasses of the cold beverage. They split the spinach and mushroom pizza with added pepperoni.

As they were leaving, Ravyn was holding her chest.

"What's wrong?" Marc asked.

"That pepperoni gave me heartburn. Ugh, I feel awful," she replied. "And my stomach is upset, too."

"That's never happened before, has it?"

"No. Maybe it was spicier than usual."

"Maybe. I didn't think it was spicier, though."

"I'll take some antacid when we get home. I'll be fine."

Two weeks later, Ravyn was wondering when her period was going to come. She was never late. She started to worry that maybe Julie was right.

She still wasn't feeling all that well, especially in the mornings, but usually felt better later in the day.

Ravyn stood up and walked to her office door and closed it. She didn't want a co-worker to overhear her conversation.

"Hey, Ravyn, what's up?" Julie asked.

"I think I need to buy a pregnancy test."

Julie was silent, then asked, "Do you think you *are* pregnant?"

"I'm not sure, but I should have had my period this week and I haven't gotten it. And since I've been on the pill, my period comes like clockwork. All your talk about the antibiotics and the queasiness I've been feeling makes me worried. I just want to know for sure."

"Go get the test."

"Can I come over to your house and do it? I don't want to do it at my house. I don't want Marc to find the test. I don't want to freak him out."

"OK, come over tonight, but stop at the store for a test."

"I'll stop at CVS on my way up. Thanks."

Chapter 16

Ravyn stopped at CVS and bought the pregnancy test. She went to the one in Midtown and prayed she wouldn't see anyone she knew. This was the one she used when she lived right up the street.

She knew the store layout and so stopped there to shop but had to search several aisles before she found the pregnancy tests. Ravyn nervously paid for the test and drove to Julie's Buckhead home.

Julie's daughters Ashley and Lexie were excited to see her and wanted Ravyn to come up to their rooms to see their new tennis racquets.

Ravyn dutifully climbed the stairs to their rooms and oohed and aahed over their junior-sized racquets. Then she climbed down the stairs to meet Julie in the kitchen.

"What do I need to do?" Ravyn asked.

"Do you have to pee?"

"Not really. I'm kind of nervous."

Julie walked to her cabinets and pulled down a clear drinking glass, filling it with filtered water from the refrigerator.

"Here, drink lots of water until you do."

Ravyn chugged two glasses of water while Julie watched in silence. They made small talk for about 15 minutes then Ravyn shook her head.

"OK, just go in the bathroom and pee on the stick. There's two in the box, so if you mess this one up, we can repeat the process and do the other test."

Ravyn disappeared into the half bath. She was so nervous. She didn't want the test to be positive.

Julie tried not to pace outside the bathroom door while Ravyn was in there, but she felt Ravyn was in there longer than necessary.

Gently, Julie knocked on the door. "Ravyn, are you OK?"

"Noooooo!" came Ravyn's wail.

"Can I come in?" Julie asked.

Ravyn sobbed as she came out of the bathroom with the pregnancy test and showed the plus sign to Julie.

Julie wrapped Ravyn in a bear hug and steered her over to the living room couch. Ravyn couldn't stop crying, and Julie just let her cry on her shoulder, holding her as tight as she could.

"What are you going to do, Ravyn?" Julie whispered.

Ravyn sat up and wiped the tears out of her eyes with the back of her hands. Julie handed her a facial tissue and Ravyn blew her nose, then tried to figure out what to do with the dirty tissue.

Julie took it from her. "I've dealt with a lot worse."

Ravyn gave Julie a sad smile.

"What are you going to do now?" Julie asked again.

"I'm going to have it. Of course, I'm going to have it," Ravyn said. Then she began to cry again. "This wasn't the way it was supposed to be! I'm not even married!"

Julie held Ravyn close again, rubbing her back. "Sweetheart, you are not the first woman who got pregnant before a wedding and you certainly won't be the last."

Ravyn sat up, a thought striking her. "I've got to tell Marc. What am I going to tell him?

"Tell him the truth. Tell him he's going to be a father."

After Ravyn calmed down and stopped crying, Julie walked her out to her Honda.

"Are you OK to drive?" Julie asked.

"I'm OK," Ravyn said, hugging Julie close. "Thank you for being here for me."

"Of course, Ravyn. You were here for me when I needed you for my surgery and I'm here for you. That's how it is for best friends. And we're not just best friends. I feel like you are my sister. I think of you as my sister."

"I feel the same way, Julie. I love you so much."

"And I love you. Now leave before I start crying."

Ravyn got in her car and headed south on Peachtree Road toward the Garden Hills home. She began crying again but drove on autopilot. She pulled into the driveway and just stared at the front door from her car.

How was she going to tell Marc? Would he be angry? Was this her fault? What if he didn't want a baby this soon, before they were even married?

She tried to screw up her courage and got out of the car and up the steps. Every step she took up the three short stairs seemed heavy.

Ravyn opened the front door.

"Hey, you're late tonight," Marc said from the kitchen. "Did you have to work late?"

Marc came out of the kitchen and looked at Ravyn. He could tell she had been crying. "What's wrong?"

"I'm pregnant," Ravyn whispered, then she began to sob again.

Marc stood stone still, shocked. "Are you sure? How do you know?"

"I am. I took the test."

"Oh my God!" he said, wrapping Ravyn in his arms. "Well, this is unexpected, but it's great news, right?"

"What are we going to do?" Ravyn asked. "I'm not supposed to be pregnant! I'm not even married yet!"

"We can still get married. I guess sooner rather than later."

"How?"

"I assume we can get married at the Fulton County Courthouse."

Ravyn began to cry harder. "My family won't be there!"

"Ravyn, Ravyn," Marc said, stroking her back. "I know it's not the wedding we were going to plan, the wedding you wanted. We don't even have our wedding bands yet."

"Can we at least get some rings?" Ravyn squeaked.

"I assume we can get some rings at Macy's or somewhere."

Ravyn shook her head. She irrationally thought she did not want to be married without wedding rings.

"I know this is not the big wedding you wanted, but I want you to be my wife. And now the mother of my child."

Marc hugged her closer. "I love you so much. It hurts me sometimes."

Ravyn smiled through her tears.

"I'm going to have to call my family tonight to let them know."

"OK, I should probably call my mother tonight, too. So, do you want to try to get married this week?"

"Don't we need a license?"

"Oh, God! The license. I'll go online and see if we can get that quickly. If we can't, can we get married next week? Is that OK?"

"Can I call Julie?" Ravyn asked, as she began crying again. "I want Julie to be there."

"Call Julie. See if she can be ready sometime this week, or next week. I'll let you know when I find out about the license."

"You'll need a best man, won't you?"

Marc frowned. "Well, I'm not sure if I can find one."

"What about your brother, Bruce?"

Marc blanched. "Bruce? I'm not so sure…"

"Marc, he's really the reason we are together."

"OK, I'll try to call him."

"Don't try, do it. Please. For me?"

Marc shook his head. He couldn't believe he'd be calling his addict brother, or former addict brother, to be his best man. But for Ravyn, he'd do it. He'd do just about anything to make her happy.

"OK, let's do it," Ravyn said, adamantly. "Oh, shit! I don't have a dress, Marc!"

"Can you get a white sundress at Macy's? You know, when we get our rings?"

"I guess so. If not, I'll just wear a white T-shirt and white running shorts. This isn't a conventional wedding after all."

Ravyn's hands shook as she dialed the number of her sister's cell phone. What would she say? How could she tell her she was pregnant and her wedding plans were ruined. She'd now have to be married at the courthouse. This was not the way she wanted things to turn out.

But she wanted to talk to Jane before she called her parents. Jane would be sympathetic to her plight, she felt sure.

Jane answered her cell and Ravyn burst into tears.

"What's wrong? Are mom and dad alright? Are you alright?"

"I'm pregnant!" Ravyn squeaked out.

"What? Oh my God! So am I!" Jane exclaimed.

"You are?"

"Yes, we've been waiting to tell everyone after the three-month mark. How far along are you? Are you excited?"

"I just took the test. I think I'm about a month along."

"Oh," Jane replied, flatly. "Oh, Ravyn. You need to call your doctor to be sure. Some of those tests can be wrong."

"Really? I thought they were reliable."

"Well, my friend Erin took one, and it said she was pregnant, but then she went to the doctor and it turned out she wasn't. Or she might have been pregnant but by the time she got into her doctor's office, she wasn't anymore. She'd had an early miscarriage and didn't even know it."

"I didn't know that could happen," Ravyn said, her mind whirling.

"Erin said her doctor said it's quite common early on in a pregnancy, so go to your doctor to be sure."

"Oh, I will! Maybe I'm not pregnant!" Ravyn said with enthusiasm.

"You don't want to be pregnant? Marc's not happy?"

"No, he says he's happy. I'd rather not be pregnant right now. I want a wedding like you had. I want all the right steps. Babies can come later."

"OK, but if you are pregnant, you'll keep it?" Jane asked.

"Yes. If I am pregnant, I will have the baby. But maybe I'm not. I'd really like to not be pregnant."

"OK. For your sake, then, I hope you aren't."

"But I'm excited for you and Nick. When are you due? "

"Right before Christmas. Around December 15."

"A Christmas baby!"

"Yes. We're very excited. It's a little sooner than we wanted, but it will be fine."

"Are you going to find out the sex of the baby?"

"We're debating that. I want to know so I can fix up the nursery with the right colors, but Nick thinks he might want to be surprised."

"You'll figure it out, I'm sure. I'm going to be an auntie!" Ravyn exclaimed.

As soon as Ravyn hung up with her sister, she called out to Marc in the other room.

"Hey! Good news. There's a chance I may not be pregnant!" Ravyn said, finding Marc in the guest bedroom, talking into his cell.

Marc looked up. "I'll call you back," he said. "What? Now you're not pregnant? I just told my mother you were."

"Oh, sorry. I talked to Jane and she said these home pregnancy tests aren't always reliable. That I should see my doctor to be sure. You told your mother I was pregnant?"

"Well, yes, because that's what you said. I thought we were telling our parents."

"Since I talked to Jane, I'm not going to tell anyone else until I'm sure."

"You don't want to be pregnant?" Marc asked, disappointed.

Ravyn reached over and took Marc's hand. "If I am pregnant, I'll have the baby. But if I'm not pregnant we can get married in a real wedding with our families around us. A real wedding ceremony. Not one down at the courthouse with strangers around me."

Marc could see Ravyn's eyes light up when she talked about a "real wedding ceremony" and realized he'd have to try to give her that, even if she was pregnant.

"What do I tell my mother?"

"Tell her I may be mistaken with the home test. I'll go to the doctor and see if I really am pregnant."

"OK, but I still want to marry you," he said. "Pregnant or not, I'm still marrying you. The sooner the better in my book."

Chapter 17

Ravyn waited nervously in her doctor's exam room. Marc had offered to come to the doctor's office with her, but she said she'd be fine. Now she wished he had come for moral support.

Her doctor performed a blood test, then had her get up in the stirrups for a pelvic exam. Ravyn wasn't ready for that. She thought it would just be a blood test. After the pelvic exam she got dressed and was waiting in the chair when the doctor came back into the exam room.

"Well, you are pregnant, Ravyn," her doctor confirmed.

Ravyn could feel her eyes begin to water.

"I take it this is an unplanned pregnancy?" her doctor asked.

"Well, yes, but it's just that I'm not married yet. I am engaged to be married."

"We can talk about options if you'd like to end the pregnancy," the doctor said.

"No, no! I'll have the baby. I want the baby. This just isn't the order I expected. How far along am I?"

"Based on what you've told me, I'd say you are close to two months along." The doctor took out a wheel and spun it around, looking for the 40-week mark. "Your due date should be about February 18 of next year."

Ravyn counted on her fingers to the month of February. "Are you sure? I had my period in early June."

"You can have some light bleeding in your first trimester. You didn't have one after that, though, correct?"

"Correct."

"Then I suspect your due date is in mid-February." The doctor reached over for a pre-printed pregnancy booklet, handing it to Ravyn. "You'll need an OB/GYN now and I can make some recommendations."

Ravyn numbly shook her head. She was pregnant. She was hoping against hope that she hadn't been. That the home test had been wrong.

"Here's a list of some nearby OB/GYNs, but you can choose your own, obviously," the doctor said, taking out another pre-printed sheet and handing it to Ravyn. "Your OB/GYN can answer any questions you might have, so be sure to select one soon. You are young and healthy, so I expect this to be a routine pregnancy. You don't have any factors that would make this a high-risk pregnancy. You exercise, and you should continue to exercise as long as you can. You said you are a runner, and I'm not discouraging you from continuing that. Just know it may become uncomfortable later in your pregnancy. Listen to your body. You might find walking will be more comfortable, eventually. Congratulations, Ravyn."

Ravyn smiled weakly. "Thank you."

"Well?" Marc asked, when Ravyn called him from the parking deck of the doctor's office.

"I am pregnant."

"That's wonderful, Ravyn! I mean, I know this isn't the way we wanted to start our marriage, but you'll see, Ravyn. It will be OK. When are you due?"

"February 18, according to my doctor. I have to find an OB/GYN now. I wanted to find a wedding dress first," Ravyn said, starting to cry again.

"Oh honey, we'll get you a wedding dress. Maybe we can get married in the backyard. I looked it up and we can get the license pretty quickly."

"In late July? I'll stroke out from the heat and humidity. At least the courthouse will be air conditioned."

"Maybe we can find another place with air conditioning."

"We'll never find anything so soon," she said through her tears. "We're going to have to get married at the courthouse."

"Maybe not. Let me find out what our options are. Come home and we'll go from there."

Ravyn drove home, a million thoughts in her head. Was she ready to be a mother? Would she be a good mother? What was the baby going to do to hers and Marc's relationship? It had suffered a crisis when she took off for Mexico.

She didn't know what she would have done if Marc hadn't come looking for her. She could have ended up in a very bad situation with that Sandy guy.

Ravyn didn't really ask herself if Marc would be a good father. She felt she knew the answer to that one: He would. She tried to think of why she felt so sure about that, when she had doubts about herself as a mother.

As Ravyn pulled up to the driveway, she tried to banish any doubts from her mind. She was having the baby and she'd just have to learn to be a good mother. After all, she could always ask her own mother for advice, or Julie.

Ravyn planned to call her parents later that night to give them the news. No more putting it off. She'd text Jane, since Jane already knew she likely was pregnant.

Jane. Ravyn smiled that she and her sister were going to be pregnant at the same time. Her child would at least have one cousin the same age.

Ravyn sat in her car in the driveway remembering all the fun she'd had as a kid with her cousins, who were all about the same age. There was Jody, Jimmy, Joe David, Peter and Trisha. They were all thick as thieves when they got together for a week during summer vacations.

Marc stuck his head out of the front door. "Everything OK?"

"Yes," Ravyn answered, getting out of her car. "I was just thinking how it will be great for our child to have a cousin the same age."

Marc looked quizzically at her. "A cousin?"

"I told you Jane was pregnant, too."

"Oh, right. I thought you were talking about my sister Brooke's kids. They will be older cousins, of course. Are you hungry? I can start dinner."

"I think I am a bit hungry. I want to look through the stuff the doctor gave me. One is a beginner's pregnancy guide and the other is a list of OB/GYNs. I've got to pick one out. Maybe I'll ask Julie who her doctor is."

"Sounds like a good idea. Want a glass of wine?" Marc asked, without thinking.

"I can't, Marc. I can't have any alcohol from here on out until the baby's born."

"Sorry. I should know that. Maybe I'll give it up for the duration. In solidarity."

"Marc, you don't have to do that. I know how you like your scotch."

Marc's face fell. He'd only been thinking of wine or beer, not liquor. Not his scotch. "Oh, well. Maybe I won't then."

Ravyn curled up on the brown leather sofa and began to read the booklet her doctor had given her. Felix jumped up next to her, demanding to be petted.

The booklet listed things she should do, like take prenatal vitamins, reduce stress and keep up with exercise. She'd have to remember to pick up the vitamins at the drugstore or grocery store the next time she went.

But there was a longer list of things she couldn't do: no alcohol, limit the amount of caffeine she drank, no energy drinks, no smoking, no use of recreational drugs, no soft cheeses, no heavy lifting, no saunas or hot tubs, no raw or undercooked foods including fish and eggs.

Ravyn sighed. Well, since Twist closed last fall, she and Julie hadn't had sushi in a while. She wouldn't be able to eat any sushi for a while, either.

Julie! She needed to call Julie with the official news.

"Did the rabbit die?" Julie asked when Ravyn called.

"What?"

"You know, the rabbit test. Never mind, are you pregnant?"

"I am."

"Oh, Ravyn, I'm so happy for you. When are you due?"

"Mid-February. The doctor thinks February 18. But I need to pick an OB/GYN. Who is yours? Is she accepting new patients?

"My doctor is Dr. Watkins, Brenda Watkins. I'll text you her number. I love her. Are you feeling OK?"

"I'm just a little bit tired and a lot overwhelmed."

"That's to be expected."

"Julie, do you think I'm ready to be a mother?" Ravyn said, almost in a whisper, her voice cracking.

"Ravyn, I think you will be a great mom. And if you have any questions, I'm right here. It's been several years since I've been pregnant, but I can try to answer any questions you have."

Ravyn started to cry over the phone. "I just feel so scared and uncertain."

"That's to be expected. And your hormones are all over the place. You can be fine one minute and a flood of tears the next. Better warn Marc to watch out for flying salad spinners," Julie said with a laugh.

"Salad spinners? What are you talking about?"

"Well, when I was pregnant with Lexie, Rob and I were in the kitchen. I was making a salad. He asked me something or maybe he told me something, and I got this rush of anger. I could feel it in my entire body. I just got so mad I threw the salad spinner at him. Then I burst into tears and ran out of the room."

"You threw a salad spinner at him?"

"I did. Hit him square in the chest. We kind of joke about it now. It's like it's our special code. Don't get salad spinner mad, or this might make you salad spinner mad."

Ravyn giggled despite her tears. "I'm just going down this list the doctor gave me, and it says I can't have sushi!"

"Yeah, I guess it's a good thing Twist closed, right?"

"I wouldn't go that far. But this just sucks," Ravyn looked down again at the list. "No cleaning the litter box. Crap. Marc isn't going to like that. It's always been my chore to take care of Felix and his box."

"Well, Marc's just going to have to do it from now on. I'm surprised you haven't been more upset about not having alcohol."

"I *am* upset about that. With all this stress, I'd like some right now. Now that I know I can't have wine, I feel like I'm craving a glass. Marc wanted to give up alcohol with me until he realized he'd have to give up scotch. Then he said no way."

"Well, I'll bring a bottle of champagne after you have the baby and we can all toast his or her good health."

"Sounds good. Thank you for being such a good friend. I guess I should thank you for taking away that glass of wine at Seven Lamps, too."

"Just looking out for my bestie."

"Love you, Jules. I'm so glad we are friends."

"Love you right back, Ravyn."

Ravyn walked into the kitchen, where Marc was marinating some fish for dinner. He intended to broil the salmon and serve it with brown and wild rice and some steamed asparagus spears.

"I've got some bad news with all these can'ts from this pregnancy list," Ravyn said.

"Oh, no. Is salmon on the list?"

"As long as it's not raw it's OK. No sushi, no soft cheeses, no coffee."

"No coffee?"

"Well, I am to limit my intake of caffeine."

"So, no more Starbucks for you."

"And you're going to have to take care of Felix's litter box for the duration of the pregnancy."

"Oh, hell. That's a crappy job. Get it?"

"I get it. You are a real comedian. I'm really going to miss my wine."

"How will you survive?"

"I'm thinking of taking up smoking."

"I know you're kidding, but don't even think about it. I want this baby as healthy as he or she can be. Will we know the gender?"

"I suppose we can."

"Don't you want to know beforehand?" Marc asked.

"I'm not sure. I kind of do and I kind of don't."

"We have several months to think about it. But now we need to start planning the wedding."

"If we can wait a week or so my parents might be able to come down. My sister, too. And I've got to have Julie there. Will your parents come? Your brother and sister?

"I'm not sure Brooke will fly out from Phoenix for my shotgun wedding."

"Marc, I'm not forcing you to marry me," said Ravyn, putting her hands on her hips. She was getting salad spinner mad.

"I'm sorry. That was a poor choice of words. My elopement is probably a better word."

"I think an elopement doesn't involve inviting a bunch of people to witness the ceremony."

"I do wish we could do it in the backyard."

"We've discussed this. The humidity would do a number on my hair, especially if I want to wear it in some sort of updo. I want air conditioning."

"Hey, what about sex?"

"What about sex?" an exasperated Ravyn asked.

"Is that on the can't list?"

Ravyn shook her head in amazement. Is that all men think about?

"So that's a no?" Marc asked.

"It's an 'I can't believe you are thinking about sex right now.' That is on the can list."

"Well, I'm not thinking about sex right this very minute, but I'm glad we can still have sex."

"You realize sex is what got us into this mess."

"Ravyn, this is not a mess. I'm excited we're having a baby. Aren't you excited?"

"OK, OK. This is not a mess. I'm just a little overwhelmed, Marc. I want this baby too. And this booklet says in the third trimester, sex might actually bring on labor."

"Good to know. I'll be looking forward to the third trimester."

"Of course, I'll be as big as a whale, so that might not be so attractive."

Marc wrapped his arms around Ravyn. "I don't care how big you get. You will always be beautiful to me." Marc suddenly choked up with emotion. "You are going to be the mother of my children. Our children."

Chapter 18

Ravyn was nervous as she called her mother. She talked to her mother every week and chose a Saturday to call her.

"Hi darling, how are you?" her mother, Kaye, asked.

Suddenly, Ravyn was choked up, almost unable to speak. "I'm fine," she squeaked.

"What's wrong, honey?"

"Mom, Mom," Ravyn began. "I'm, I'm pregnant."

There was a pause from her mother. It seemed endless to Ravyn.

"Oh," Kaye said.

Ravyn began to cry.

"Oh, honey, don't cry. Is Marc supportive?"

"He is. He's happy about the baby. It's just not how I wanted this to happen. We're going to have to move up the wedding. Like in the next few weeks."

"You let us know, and your father and I would love to be there."

Ravyn began crying harder. "I don't know how to tell Dad."

"You let me tell him."

"I feel so embarrassed. Who gets pregnant before their wedding?"

"Well," Kaye said. "Your great-grandmother did."

"What?"

"Your great-grandmother got pregnant before her wedding."

Ravyn had vague memories of her great-grandmother. A salt-of-the-earth woman who spent her whole life in Nebraska. She'd even heard stories she'd been born in a sod house, and how she and her great-grandfather had plotted out their land as a homestead, real pioneers.

"Great-grandma Alma was pregnant before she got married?"

"She was. Had to get married quickly."

Ravyn smiled thinking of her great-grandmother. She remembered her as a petite, spry, bright woman. She remembered dressing up in her shoes and dresses as a young girl. She had such small feet! She recalled she had stylish dresses, for a woman of her time, and had a mink coat.

"Well, I guess if it was OK for Alma, it will be OK for me," Ravyn said, trying to sound cheerful.

"Of course, it will be OK," Kaye said. "Ravyn, as long as Marc loves you and will be supportive, it will be OK. And even if he didn't, we love you. We'd take care of you."

"Oh, Mom," Ravyn's voice cracked again. "Thank you. He does love me and he is supportive. We'll be OK."

"Do you know your due date?"

"Mid-February. The doctor told me February 18, but I need to pick an OB/GYN and reconfirm that."

"I can't believe you and your sister are going to make me a grandmother so soon!" Now Kaye began to cry.

"What's wrong?"

"I can't be a grandmother! I'm too young!"

Ravyn couldn't help but laugh. "Oh, Mom. You'll be a fabulous grandmother. You and Dad are both so young and will be able to enjoy your grandkids."

"Have you gotten a wedding dress yet?" Kaye asked, turning more practical.

"No. Not yet. And I need to get one really soon so when I get married, I don't show."

Ravyn began crying again. "I don't know whether to have a bridal shower or a baby shower. This just sucks."

"Ravyn, don't say that. Listen, just have a baby shower. You and Marc likely have everything you need since you blended two households. But you don't have anything for a baby, do you?"

"No, we don't have anything. We need to set up a nursery. I guess we'll do it in one of the guest rooms. We don't have a crib or anything."

"So do a baby shower and you'll get most of what you need. Your father and I can get your crib. We'd love to get that for you, or your bassinet. Do couples still get a bassinet?"

"I have no idea. I guess I'll go online and see what the trends are for expectant couples."

"Well, Target has nice things."

"Yeah, there's other baby stores. I'll let you know what we pick. Right now, I need to get the wedding dress."

"I love you, Ravyn," Kaye said, her voice cracking again. "I can tell you are upset but know that God will work this out. Trust in Him."

"I will. Love you, Mom."

Ravyn called her sister, Jane, next.

"Jane, I got tested by my doctor. I am pregnant."

"That's great! Isn't it great we are both pregnant at the same time? When are you due?"

"Mid-February. The doctor told me February 18."

"So just a couple of months after me."

"Yes."

"I'm so excited for you. Are you excited? Is Marc excited?"

"He is. I think he was shocked, but then so was I. We've got to push up the wedding, like have it in a couple of weeks. Jane, do you think you can come down to Atlanta to stand up for me?"

"Of course, Ravyn. You know I'll be there for you. You just let me know when I need to be there. Do you have a venue?"

"Marc and I thought initially we'd get married at the courthouse. Then he suggested the backyard of our home. I'm not sure I want the ceremony in the backyard in August. The heat and humidity will be awful."

"Well, maybe it won't be so bad."

"Ugh, I just told him we should get married in the courthouse where it is air conditioned."

"A backyard wedding might be nice though. You could put a tent up so it would be shaded. And rent those big fans."

"Oh, yeah. Maybe we could do that. Just plan on a sleeveless dress. No sense in you being uncomfortable too."

"Ravyn, it will be OK.'

"Mom said the same thing."

"Well listen to her and me. It will be OK."

"Love you, Jane. I'm so lucky to have you as my sister."

"Love you, too, big sister. I hit the jackpot with you."

"Ha! You didn't think that when we were teenagers!"

"Well, Ravyn, we were teenagers."

Ravyn just laughed. "You are so right."

Ravyn called Julie the next day and asked if she could go shopping for a wedding dress with her next Saturday.

"Of course! Have you gone online to look, too?"

"I have. There's a really nice white sleeveless dress at J. Crew. That's kind of my backup dress. It's not that expensive either. But I'm hoping I can find one locally. Maybe at a retail store where I can try it on, make sure it fits and I don't look horrible in it."

"Are you starting to show? You shouldn't be showing yet. You should look fine in a dress."

"I suppose I'll look OK in the next couple of weeks. Will you just come for moral support?"

"Of course, I will. Why don't I come pick you up early Saturday and we can hit a few specialty shops and maybe even some bridal shops. I'll do whatever you need me to. Have you picked a wedding date?"

"We're debating August 13 or August 20. Honestly, it kind of depends on if I find a dress. I think Marc is just planning to rent a tux. Then again, he's got some nice suits. He could just wear one of those."

"He'd look great in a tux. Make him rent one."

"Julie, I've asked my sister to stand up for me, but I'd really like you to stand up for me, too. Can you do that? Will you do that?"

"Ravyn," Julie started to say, her voice cracking. "I'd be honored. Do you have a color for your bridesmaid's dress?"

"Oh, I didn't even think of that. Honestly, I didn't tell Jane what color to pick. I'll tell her to select summer colors. Pastels or something. You do the same. And sleeveless since we're thinking of holding the ceremony in the backyard. Don't worry. Jane told me to rent a tent and some big fans."

"You better rent a full-sized cooler for me. Since I've had my surgery, I am the queen of hot flashes."

"And do you think the girls would still want to be flower girls?" Ravyn asked. "Even if it's in the backyard?"

"Oh my God. They would love that! I'll get them some cute matching dresses. I can't wait to tell them. They are going to be over the moon that you want them to be in your wedding. You know they adore you."

When Ravyn got off the phone with Julie, she realized she'd need to ask Marc to select another groomsman. She knew he was planning to ask his brother Bruce to be his best man, but he'd have to ask someone else so there'd be an even number since she'd asked Julie.

"Marc, I've asked Julie to stand up for me, too," Ravyn said. "Is there someone else you can ask to be another groomsman?"

"I can ask Clay O'Connor."

"Who is Clay O'Connor? "

"He was my best friend in college, at UGA, in law school."

"Why haven't I met him? You've never even talked about him."

"He lives in Savannah now. He's an attorney there. I've never talked about him because I hardly ever see him. We've sort of lost touch. He may not be able to stand up for me on short notice," Marc said. Then he paused, saying, "He was my best man for my first wedding. If you'd rather I not ask him, I'd understand."

"If he's your best friend from college, you should invite him."

"OK, I'll call him. It will be good to catch up."

Marc went into the den and called Clay, coming out about a half hour later.

"Good news, Clay said he'd love to be there for the wedding."

"Great! We just need to find someone to marry us. I'm warming to the idea of getting married in the backyard. Get it, warming?" Ravyn laughed.

"Good thing I'm not marrying you for your standup comedy skills."

"Did you talk to your sister and brother? Will they be coming to the wedding?"

"I've talked to Brooke. She was looking at flights. Thankfully, Southwest has pretty cheap flights so she might be able to make it."

"I'm really excited to meet her."

"I think you two will really get along. She reminds me a lot of you."

"Eww."

"Not like that. I'm just saying you two have the same kind of personalities."

"And have you talked to your brother?"

"I've left several messages, but I haven't heard from him. Even my mother hasn't heard from him. It's not a good sign. He's probably using again."

Ravyn was silent. "But he seemed so together at Christmas."

187

"Well, that was Christmas," Marc spat. "You don't know my brother, Bruce. He's been in and out of rehab. We, well, my mom, always hopes he's turned the corner, but he never does. Honey, I don't think we should count on him at the wedding, or as my best man. Clay can be at the wedding. I can ask him to be my best man. He's excited to meet you."

"Don't give up on your brother just yet. Maybe he's just busy."

"Busy getting high or drunk."

"Marc."

"Don't Marc me. You didn't grow up with him and watch him spiral out of control. It started in high school and he just went down from there. Years of abusing drugs. It's a wonder he's not dead. You don't know him and what he is. I do."

"OK, but I'm going to give him the benefit of the doubt."

"Well, Ravyn, you are going to be disappointed. You can't give Bruce the benefit of the doubt."

Ravyn and Julie were at their fourth bridal shop in Buckhead, having been to La Maison de la Bridal, Brides by Demetrios, and Dress the Bride. They were now at David's Bridal. And when they were done, they planned to head around the corner to Seven Lamps for a late lunch.

Ravyn fell in love with a strapless chiffon wedding dress with a ruched bodice, which would sort of hide her small tummy. And the dress was under $300. She couldn't believe her luck. She couldn't believe she was going to be able to buy a wedding dress off the rack that would fit and didn't need an alteration.

Ravyn and Julie were practically giddy with excitement when they got to Seven Lamps.

"I can't believe I found a dress!" Ravyn exclaimed as they sat down at their table.

"And you look great in it. I'm jealous you found one so inexpensive. Mine cost close to $1,000! And that's without any alterations."

"Well, I just hope I'm not showing by August 27. We've had to move to that weekend because Marc's sister Brooke got a flight on that weekend. We still haven't heard from Marc's brother Bruce, but you can be there, my parents and my sister and her husband can be there and Marc's parents can be there. We got the tent. We got the fans. We got a florist to do some flowers at the altar. We've catered the food. Everything is last minute and is costing us a bit more. I just pray nothing goes wrong."

"Oh, sweetie, something will always go wrong on a wedding day."

"Don't say that! Don't jinx me!"

"God, you don't know how my wedding went wrong!"

"Really? It went wrong?"

"Oh, yes. For one, it rained, so my hair got all frizzy. Then I got my period and I was afraid it was going to go through my tampon and stain my dress. And then the heel of my dress shoe broke during our first dance!"

"I never realized that."

"I wish I'd known you then. You are so calm, cool and collected you would have made sure it went right."

Ravyn barked out a laugh. "You are delusional. I am not calm, cool nor collected. I feel like I'm a hot mess these days."

"That's probably the pregnancy hormones working overtime."

Suddenly Julie began to cry. Ravyn took her hand across the table.

"Julie, what's wrong?"

"I'm sorry. I'm a hot mess, too, with menopause. I'm just so sad that I can't have any more children. I know Rob and I are really done with our family, but I see you and…"

Ravyn went wide eyed. "Oh, Julie, I'm sorry."

"No, I'm happy for you. I really am," she said, squeezing Ravyn's hand back. "But I'm just sad for me."

"Of course, of course you are. I can't imagine how hard this is for you."

Julie pulled her hand away and wiped her eyes with the back of her hand. "I don't want to make this about me, Ravyn. I'm really happy we found your dress today and I'm excited you are having a baby. Listen," she said, trying to be serious. "My tween daughters have discovered the mall and want to buy everything. They are going to need their own pocket money and they will be able to babysit for you."

Ravyn tipped her head back and laughed. "Built in babysitters! I love it!"

Ravyn got back to the house and charged into the kitchen, excited to tell Marc her news about the wedding dress.

"I found the perfect dress!" she exclaimed. "I can't wait for you to see it on the wedding day!"

"I can't wait to see you in it that day, too. Thanks for being flexible about the wedding date. I know it's been a moving target."

"I want your sister to be there, Marc. Have you heard from your brother, yet?"

"He texted me today, actually. Says he'll be there. I'm not holding my breath though, Ravyn. He's disappointed me and my family way too many times. I've asked Clay to be my best man. We may not have an even number if Bruce doesn't show. Is that OK?"

Ravyn frowned, thinking there would be an odd number, then brightened and smiled. "Really, we just need to get married."

"We need to get our marriage license."

"We do. When should we go get it?"

"We can go this week. I can meet you for lunch one day and we can get it downtown."

"That would be perfect. I haven't told anyone at work I'm pregnant but they know we're engaged. Of course, some of my co-workers have asked where my engagement ring went."

"Speaking of which, I did return to Tiffany's for another ring." Marc reached into his pants pocket and pulled out another Tiffany blue ring box.

"Oh, Marc! You didn't!"

"Ravyn, will you marry me, again?" Marc asked, getting down on his knee and presenting a second ring to her.

"Oh, Marc!" Ravyn pulled out the new engagement ring. It was a round diamond ring with diamonds around the center diamond itself. "It's beautiful!"

"I know it's not what you had before," Marc stammered. "But I thought we needed a new start."

Ravyn could feel tears come to her eyes. "We do," she choked.

"I picked out sapphires and diamonds for our wedding bands. I hope that's OK. They'll be ready by our wedding date."

"You picked out the wedding bands?"

"Well, yes. We needed them, right? Sooner rather than later."

"Yes. But you have sapphires on your wedding band? I thought you picked out a plain band."

"That was before. Sapphires are your favorite gemstone, right?"

"Yes."

"Well then, it's now my favorite gemstone. I want to look down at my ring and be reminded of our bond. I want to be a part of you, Ravyn."

Ravyn broke down and cried in Marc's arms.

Chapter 19

Marc and Ravyn booked a block of hotel rooms at the Mandarin Oriental in Buckhead for their wedding guests, paying for everything, so their guests wouldn't have to. Ravyn even convinced Julie to book a room in the hotel so she and her husband could have the vacation they missed back on Memorial Day weekend.

Julie called her parents in Florida, asking them to drive up to Atlanta for the wedding weekend to watch Lexie and Ashley.

To Julie's surprise they agreed, delighted to spend time with their granddaughters. Julie would just have to be sure her parents got the girls dressed and ready to be Ravyn's flower girls.

Julie had found cute pale pink sundresses for both of her daughters and then found a strapless sundress in almost the same color for herself. Once again Julie was grateful for what she could find at Nordstrom.

As the wedding day drew closer, Ravyn could feel her anxiety begin to build. What if it rained that day? What if it was too hot? What if the minister didn't show up? What if Bruce didn't show up? What if, what if, what if.

She also didn't want Marc to know she was having lots of morning sickness. She was hiding it pretty well, usually not getting sick until she got to her office downtown.

Her appointment with her new OB/GYN Dr. Brenda Watkins went well, and Ravyn could tell why Julie loved her. Dr. Watkins was a middle-aged woman who was petite with short brown hair with just the slightest bit of gray in it. She had a bubbly personality and she put Ravyn at ease right away.

"I'm not going to say this pregnancy will be a piece of cake," Dr. Watkins said. "You'll be cursing your husband about months eight and nine."

Ravyn laughed nervously. She'd heard some of the stories of how uncomfortable women got in the last trimester. Then she thought of Julie's salad spinner story.

"At least you won't be pregnant in the dog days of summer. Lord, I had my first child in August and I thought I would die of the heat from my body and my little incubating baby," Dr. Watkins said, patting her abdomen as if she were still pregnant. "I'd recommend those cooling sheets for your bed. They pretty much saved me and my husband."

"Oh, I'm not married," Ravyn blurted out. "Not yet anyway. The wedding's August 27. We had to move the date up so my fiancé's sister could attend."

"That's great."

Dr. Watkins confirmed Ravyn's due date, made several appointments for her, including some lab work to be done, explained when she'd need to have the ultrasound and that she and Marc could find out the gender then if they wanted.

"That's no guarantee, though," Dr. Watkins cautioned. "My boy mooned the ultrasound tech and we never did see his little penis. He came out a surprise."

Ravyn laughed as she got down from the exam table.

"Of course, that was over 20 years ago and a lot has changed since then," the doctor said. She hugged Ravyn before she left the exam room.

"We're a team now, Ravyn," Dr. Watkins said. "Don't keep anything from me. I don't expect anything to go wrong, but if something doesn't feel right, I need to know."

Dr. Watkins handed over a card with her after-hours number and a cell number.

"You give out your cell number to your patients?" Ravyn asked.

"I find they don't abuse it," she replied. "They really only call if it's an emergency. And that's not my personal cell. It's the office cell. But I want you to call it if you need to."

Ravyn left her new doctor's office hoping she'd never have to call that cell number.

Ravyn, Jane and Julie sat in Jane's hotel room the Friday before the wedding putting together wedding treat bags for their guests. Marc and Ravyn hadn't invited that many guests. They worked it out that they could seat about 50 in the backyard.

Marc had invited his family, his best man Clay O'Connor, Amy and Kyle Quitman, and a few guys from the gym. He even thought about inviting Kyle Quitman's pilot, Ryan Hays, since the pilot had gotten him to Mexico to rescue his relationship with Ravyn.

Marc couldn't suppress a smile when he thought that his and Ravyn's induction into the mile-high club on that private plane might very well be the reason for their wedding.

Ravyn had far more friends coming, some co-workers, Julie and her family, Ravyn's family and Jane and her husband Nick. When Ravyn initially looked at the white folding chairs they'd rented, along with the tent and fans, she doubted they'd need that much seating. Now she was stressing that they'd need more chairs.

"OK, each gift bag gets some sun lotion, one of these tiny electric fans, a bottle of water, and hand sanitizer," Ravyn said, holding up each item as she displayed it.

"You're no fun. Where are the tiny bottles of booze for each bag?" Julie cracked.

Ravyn and Jane both looked at her. "You realize we're both pregnant," Ravyn said. "We can't have any. And if we can't have any, no one can have any. Also, no spiking the punch."

"Party pooper," Julie smiled, throwing a small bottle of hand sanitizer at her.

"Now listen, the both of you, I don't want any arguments. I've booked appointments for you two at the Mandarin Oriental's spa. A massage, a facial, the works. You will be relaxed and glowing for the ceremony."

"What?" Jane asked. "You didn't have to do that."

"I know I didn't, but I wanted to. I love you both so much and I'm so happy you both could make it. I wanted a special treat for you."

"Ravyn, you really should come with us. You will need the spa treatment, too. I know you are acting all calm and collected, but I know when you start twirling your hair with your fingers you are nervous."

Ravyn dropped her hand from her hair. "I'm going to be bald at this rate. And who said I'm not going with you? I booked it for all of us!"

"Sweet! When do we go?" Jane asked, thinking of the dim candlelight, warm massage oils, and soft towels.

"I've booked it for 4 p.m. today, before we have to be at the rehearsal dinner. It's just our families and wedding party going to Dantana's. We've got the private room at 7 tonight."

"But aren't we doing the rehearsal before then?" Jane asked.

"Jane, we're getting married in my backyard with just close family and friends," Ravyn said. "We'll do a quick rehearsal right before the ceremony."

"Oh, OK. Is Dad paying for tonight's dinner?" Jane asked.

"I've asked him not to, but I'm not sure he'll listen. I don't expect Marc's father will chip in. He and Marc aren't on the best of terms. Quite frankly, Marc's father kind of intimidates me. I think Marc's planning to pre-pay so there's no question or argument about it."

"Good luck. You know Dad will want to pay."

"I know."

"I'm just glad my parents are here to watch the girls. It will be nice for just Rob and I to have dinner out as adults. No having to look at a kids' menu or trying to make them behave."

"Yeah, and we're close enough we can just walk over, have all the wine you want and then walk back," Ravyn said.

"When's Marc's sister coming in?" Jane asked.

"She should be getting in right about now," Ravyn said, looking down at her watch. Brooke was flying in, without her husband and children, from Phoenix and would be flying out on Sunday. It would be a short trip for her, but Ravyn was glad she could come. "Marc should be at the airport now to pick her up."

"Is she staying at the hotel, too?"

"No, she said she wanted to stay with Marc's parents since her time here is so short. I can't blame her, although we did try to talk her into staying at the hotel."

"Are you and Marc staying in the hotel after the wedding?" Julie asked.

"We are. We couldn't get the bridal suite but we have another suite. Seriously, we're not going to be paying much attention to the room," Ravyn said.

"Well, hubba hubba," Julie laughed.

Ravyn blushed. "I didn't mean it like that. I'll probably be so tired I'll just want to go to bed."

"Yeah, you will," Jane teased her sister.

"Julie and Jane, don't you both start."

"Are you feeling good with your pregnancy, Jane?" Julie asked.

"I'm feeling great. I'm right at the start of my second trimester. I have more energy and my appetite is good."

"Oh, I'm looking forward to that," Ravyn said. "I'm still feeling queasy. And it's not just in the morning. Sometimes it goes on all day. Saltines and Sprite are my new best friends."

"Yeah, I had it pretty easy with Ashley," Julie said. "But I had a much harder time with Lexie. Lots of morning sickness. You may have it rough with this pregnancy, but your next one might be completely different."

"Hey, I wasn't ready for this one!" Ravyn said. "Don't wish another one on me already!"

"Just know it's not always going to be this way," Julie tried to reassure her.

"I'm worried I'm going to be sick the day of the wedding. I've kind of hidden how sick I've been from Marc. But I may not be able to hide it if I'm puking my guts out tomorrow."

"I'll bring a breath mint for you if that happens," Julie said. "Make sure you are minty fresh when the minister says 'Marc, you may kiss the bride.'"

"OK, now I'm feeling sick," Jane said.

"Topic change, please!" Ravyn said.

"Are you going to go on any sort of honeymoon?" Jane asked.

"Well, thanks to Julie, I've had my honeymoon for one in Mexico," Ravyn said. "I'm doing the next one with my husband. We're going to drive down to St. Simons Island, to the King & Prince," she added, referring to the Georgia resort right on the beach. "We'll be there for a couple of days. It's not Tahiti like you and Nick's honeymoon, but neither one of us can take much time off on such short notice. Honestly, considering how quickly we've pulled this wedding together, we're glad to be able to get away for even a short time."

"Are you going to take his name?" Julie asked.

"I think I'm going to be a modern gal and keep my maiden name, at least for now."

"What about the baby?" Jane asked, concerned.

"What about the baby?" Ravyn asked.

"Are you going to hyphenate? Shaw-Linder?" Jane asked.

"Oh, no. It will just be Linder. I wouldn't do that to a kid."

"Have you guys even talked about baby names?" her sister asked.

"No, we haven't. And before you ask, we are unsure if we are going to find out the gender of the baby. It's too soon, I think."

"Well, you've got lots of time," Julie said.

"Have you thought about names, Jane, for your baby? And am I having a niece or a nephew?"

"Nick and I will find out the sex of the baby, for sure. We want to know. It would just kill me to wait until the birth. You know I hate surprises! We've kicked around some names, too. But we're not telling anyone the baby's name until he or she is born. That's going to be a surprise."

"Yeah, when my husband and I told everyone Lexie's name, we got a lot of opinions about it," Julie said. "Well, actually, I told everyone her name and I got a lot of grief from fellow moms about it. Told me it was 'too trendy' and everyone was naming their girls Lexie. Ugh! I wished I'd never told anyone until she was born. You're smart."

"That's *exactly* why we're not telling anyone until the birth," Jane agreed.

"Hey, look at the time! We should be down at the spa for our massages," Ravyn said.

The three women were almost late for the rehearsal dinner at Dantana's. The wedding party had a private room toward the back of the surf and turf restaurant.

Jane's husband Nick was there, along with Julie's husband Rob. Marc's parents, Carol and Edward, and Ravyn's parents, Kaye and John, were there, as was Marc's sister Brooke and his brother, Bruce.

Marc's best man, Clay O'Connor, planned to drive up from Savannah the morning of the wedding, so he wasn't at the dinner.

Marc introduced Ravyn to Brooke. "I've heard so much about you," they both said together. Then they laughed.

"I told you both I thought you'd be friends," Marc laughed along with them.

He left the women chatting amicably and walked over to his brother.

"Hey, Bruce," he said. "You know the wedding is at 3 o'clock tomorrow, right?"

"Yeah, Marc. You've only told me about a thousand times."

"I just don't want you to forget or not be there. Ravyn really wants you there."

"What about you?" Bruce asked, suspiciously.

"Me, too."

"I'll be there. And I'll be there early so we can do whatever you need. I'm borrowing a friend's car."

"A friend's car? Did you need a ride?"

"Bro, you know I don't have a car. But I have it covered."

"Do you have a driver's license?"

"Yeah, Marc," Bruce said, angry now. "I have a license. Don't worry, I'll be there."

Marc's mother, Carol came up to Bruce's side and began talking to her youngest son. Marc walked away from their conversation shaking his head. He wasn't so sure his brother did have a valid driver's license.

Marc walked over to hear Ravyn's father, John, explaining to his father, Edward, how he had once owned a tire store, then sold insurance, then became a business professor at Clemson University.

"That's a lot of careers," Edward Linder said. "I've only ever been a lawyer. My son was a lawyer once, too, for the best law firm in Atlanta, before he threw it all away for his little pet project. A technology company. What does he know about technology? He's a lawyer. He's lucky someone wanted to buy that company from him."

John looked at Edward with discomfort. He then looked at Marc quizzically.

"Come on, Dad, don't talk me down to the bride's father. John, here, might tell Ravyn she can do better," Marc said, trying to lighten the mood.

"Well, I'm not so sure she couldn't do better," Edward said, walking away to find his wife, Carol.

"Sorry, John. As you can see, my father doesn't think all that much of me," Marc said.

John put his hand on Marc's shoulder. "I will be proud to call you my son-in-law. I don't think Ravyn could find a better man than you."

Marc looked at John, swallowing the lump in his throat. "Thank you," he whispered. "That means a lot to me."

Ravyn and Marc fell into bed that night, exhausted. "Dear God, this day seemed to go on forever," Marc said.

"It felt like a long day because it was. Although I had a massage in the afternoon, so I got some relaxation. You had to drive to the airport and spend time with your mom and dad after you dropped Brooke off at their house."

"Don't remind me. It was great being with my mom and sister, but I wish my dad could just be happy for us. For me."

"I'm sorry, Marc. I could tell tonight was strained between you and your father."

"Strained is the nicest word for it. He's really being an ass. And my brother, Jesus!"

"What about Bruce?"

"He says he's borrowed someone's car to be at the wedding tomorrow. I'm not sure he has a driver's license, though. Ravyn, I wouldn't count on him tomorrow. I know you want him there. I'm not sure why."

"Marc," she said, rolling over on her side. "He's your brother. It sounds like he's trying. Although if he needed a ride, we could have gotten an Uber for him."

"I wouldn't have gotten an Uber for him," Marc said, pulling Ravyn close.

"Well, I would have. I'm hoping that years from now you'll be happy he was there. The family photos will be of all of our families."

"I love that you are so optimistic."

"I just want you to be happy."

"I'll be happy tomorrow when I say, 'I do,'" Marc said, kissing her forehead. "Do you want to make love tonight?"

"Hmmm," Ravyn said from the back of her throat.

"Is that a yes?"

"It's not a no. I better take advantage of it while I'm not feeling queasy."

"You barely ate anything tonight."

"I just didn't want to eat and then be sick. Or feel sick."

Marc pulled Ravyn on top of him. "It will be the last time we can make love as single people. We'll be old married farts tomorrow."

"Speak for yourself. Although I'll be a pregnant married fart tomorrow."

"You'll be my pregnant wife… ah, I won't say you'll be a fart."

"Well, I looked it up in the pregnancy book I picked up. I think I will be a big fart at some point."

"All this talk of bodily functions is making me hot," Marc said.

Ravyn giggled but could feel Marc getting hard under her. She rolled off him, kissing him, searching for his tongue.

Marc pulled back to look at her. "I love you, Ravyn," Marc whispered. "I'll never stop loving you."

Chapter 20

The morning dawned warm and humid. Ravyn hadn't slept well, a combination of nerves and morning sickness. She'd been up since before dawn downing saltines and Sprite. She'd have to keep both close today.

Ravyn sat at the small bistro table in the breakfast area of the home, when Marc came out of the bedroom.

"You OK? I didn't realize you weren't in bed."

"I couldn't really sleep. Too nervous about the day and I'm feeling queasy again."

"Anything I can do?" Marc asked, rubbing Ravyn's shoulder. He then moved around her and began massaging her neck. "God, you are tense. I'd suggest some stress-release exercises, but I know we have a tight schedule today."

"Yeah, I don't have time for that. Maybe after the wedding. I'm guessing I'll need some stress release tonight."

"I'm counting on it," Marc said. "I want some proper wedding sex."

Ravyn turned to look up at him. "I'll need to get ready later this morning. Are you going to your parents to get ready?"

"Are you kicking me out?"

"Well, I don't want you to see me before the ceremony."

"Ravyn, we're having a short rehearsal before the ceremony. I'm going to see your wedding dress."

"No, you won't. Julie let me borrow a sundress that I can quickly change out of. You won't see the wedding dress until my father starts to walk me down the aisle."

"You don't believe all that superstitious nonsense, do you?"

"Listen, I'm not saying I do or do not believe that we shouldn't see each other before the ceremony, but I'm also not taking any chances. I don't want bad juju."

"Bad juju? No such thing."

"Dammit, you probably just gave us bad juju by saying there's no such thing as bad juju."

Marc kissed the top of Ravyn's head. "Silly girl. But I will leave about 10 a.m. and get ready at my folks' house. Brooke is going to pick me up so I'll leave my car here."

"That will be nice. You two will get to spend more time together."

"She really likes you."

"Really? We didn't get to spend too much time together last night."

"She told me what she spent with you, she enjoyed."

"You won't be late getting back will you? How long will it take you to get back from Dunwoody?"

"I won't be late," he said, wrapping his arms around her. "I will be here on time to meet you at the altar. What time are Jane and Julie getting here?"

"I think they will be here around noon. The florists will be here around noon, too, to set up the flowers at the altar. I got calla lilies in some tall vases to place on the sides of the altar. The caterers are bringing some box lunches for us. There are extras for anyone who comes early."

"Julie and Jane will help you get ready?"

"I don't have to do that much, really. They'll help me with my hair and makeup."

"I'll be back by noon then, too. Save me a boxed lunch."

"I think there's chicken or beef, or vegetarian, so tell me what you want now so I can hide it in the fridge."

"What's the beef choice?"

"It's a roast beef sandwich with chips, a pickle and an apple, I think."

"That doesn't sound that exciting. What's the chicken option?"

"Chicken salad, chips, pickle and an apple."

"Seriously? That sounds even less appetizing."

"Marc, the caterers will have a nicer spread for our wedding guests. You'll get heavy hors d'oeuvres and prime rib later this afternoon. This will just tide you over and keep me from passing out."

"OK, save me the roast beef. I'm going to hop in the shower. Care to join me?" Marc said, arching an eyebrow at her.

Ravyn looked into Marc's hazel eyes. She loved looking into those eyes with the gold flecks in his irises. She sighed. Shower sex would make her late. She followed him into the large walk-in shower in the master bathroom.

Marc gently soaped up Ravyn with a soft poof. His wavy brown hair was plastered against his head as the shower rained down on him. Ravyn held his erection, moving her hand up and down, getting him even more excited.

Marc massaged between Ravyn's legs, watching her gasp with pleasure. "Tell me you want me now, Ravyn," he whispered in her ear.

"I want you now."

Marc then pressed Ravyn against the shower's glass wall, thrusting upward into her soft spaces. Her left hand left a palm print against the fogged up glass as she braced herself to his thrusts. Her right hand was wrapped around Marc's neck.

"Oh, God!" Ravyn shouted, as she neared climax. "Marc! Oh, God, Marc!"

"Ravyn, Ravyn," Marc repeated. He issued a throaty growl then barked his orgasmic release.

Ravyn's legs felt like jelly and she slumped to the shower floor. She tried to catch her breath, feeling sexually spent. Marc knelt down beside her, the lukewarm spray of the double shower head raining down on them.

Marc sat on the floor next to Ravyn, wrapping his arms around her, even as the water began to run cold. Then he ran his hand over her abdomen. "My baby lives here," he said. "My baby," he said, looking in her blue gray eyes. "Our baby."

"Marc, I'm cold."

He stood up, turned off the water, picked Ravyn up and carried her out of the shower. They were both dripping wet and the air conditioner chilled them both. Ravyn had gooseflesh all over her body. Setting her down on her feet, Marc wrapped her in a soft plush white towel. "Better?"

"Better. What time is it?"

Marc looked at his Apple watch. "It's 9 o'clock already."

"Oh! I've got to get dressed! The caterers will be here in a couple of hours!"

"A couple of hours? Ravyn, relax. We probably have another hour to take a nap."

"We do not have an hour. You have to leave at 10."

"A half hour, then. Come lay down next to me," he said, pulling her by the towel toward the bed.

They both flopped down on the bedcover, Marc pushing Ravyn's wet hair out of her face. "I'm so lucky I get to marry you today."

Marc left the house with his garment bag in one hand as he waved goodbye to Ravyn. He got into the car with Brooke. She'd borrowed her mother's Lexus to pick up her brother.

Ravyn stood on the porch and waved to her fiancé and his sister and then ran back into the house to be sick. When she could catch her breath, she ate more saltines and drank more Sprite. She knew it would be a long day.

Julie and Jane showed up a little before noon. Julie had a pastel multi-colored floral sundress for Ravyn to wear just before the wedding ceremony. They fussed over her hair and makeup, cried a little bit, then laughed.

Ravyn couldn't believe how lucky she'd gotten with having a sister like Jane and a best friend like Julie.

"Julie, this dress is gorgeous. You may not get it back," Ravyn gushed.

"Ha ha. You won't be able to wear it in three months!"

Ravyn's lower lip began to tremble.

"Oh no! Ravyn, I didn't mean that! Keep the dress! It's yours! Oh! I didn't mean to make you cry on your wedding day!"

"I think it's the hormones," Ravyn said, wiping her eyes. "I'm all over the place."

"Ravyn, it's OK. I was that way, too," Julie said.

"Oh, God! I cry at the littlest thing," Jane added. "I saw some sappy news item on TV about puppies being adopted and began bawling. Heaven help me when the Christmas ads begin on TV in November!"

Ravyn and Julie nodded through tears.

"We've got to get our gal ready for the wedding," Julie said, clapping her hands together. "No more tears. It's a happy day! We've got work to do!"

Guests began to arrive around 1 p.m., even though the ceremony was two hours later.

Ravyn, Jane and Julie greeted some of the guests while the caterers began doling out drinks and canapes for the next hour.

Ravyn grabbed a breaded crab cake as it went by on a caterer's platter and hoped it would stay down. Julie's sundress had pockets, which Ravyn had filled with saltines. Ravyn reached next for some saltines, stuffing them in her mouth.

Marc arrived shortly after 1 p.m. in his charcoal gray tuxedo. Julie was right about having Ravyn ask him to get one for the wedding ceremony. Marc looked strikingly sexy in a tux and Ravyn felt her panties get a little wet.

Marc turned from the arm of his sister Brooke to see Ravyn, standing alone in the floral sundress. He caught his breath at the sight of her, her makeup done perfectly and her hair in an updo.

Marc walked over to his future bride. "Hey, how are you feeling?"

"I'm doing OK. I only threw up twice today," Ravyn said with a weak smile.

Marc smiled down at her. "But you're good now? You look beautiful, by the way. That could be your wedding dress."

"Well, it's not. This is borrowed. And you look really great in your tuxedo. Really, really great."

"I'll let you take it off me later tonight," he said, wagging his eyebrows at her.

"Marc! People will hear you!"

"No one heard me except you. Hey, have you seen my brother, Bruce, yet?"

"Nope, haven't seen him."

Marc's lips grew tight before he said, "Ravyn, if he's not here yet, I'm not sure he's coming."

"Marc, I'm going to give Bruce the benefit of the doubt. I have faith in him."

Marc rolled his eyes. "I'm glad you have faith. I have none."

As if on cue, Bruce rounded the house and came into the backyard. He was dressed in a wrinkled brown suit that badly needed to be pressed.

Marc scowled at his brother. "Glad you could make it, Bruce."

"Hey, I said I'd be here. Do you have any food?"

"Food? We've got some box lunches if you're hungry," Ravyn said. "Roast beef or chicken salad?"

"It's for my dog. Roast beef I guess."

"Your dog?" Marc asked, surprised. "When did you get a dog?"

"I found him today at the gas station."

"Found him? At a gas station?" Marc asked.

"I think he's a stray. He's really skinny and I'm sure he's hungry."

"Where is he?" Ravyn asked.

"He's in the car. I'll keep him there for the wedding, obviously."

"You can't keep a dog in a car today," she said, shocked Bruce would leave a dog in a hot car. "It's going to be at least 90 today. He'll die."

"I left the windows open a crack."

"No, Bruce, you need to bring him in the house," Ravyn started to say.

"Hold on, Ravyn," Marc said, putting his hand out. "That dog probably has fleas if it's a stray. We are not bringing that mongrel into our home."

"Well we can't let it stay in the car," she said. "Do you have some rope? We could tie it to the tent stake near one of the fans. We'll get a bowl of water and it will stay cool in the shade."

"I'll go find some rope," Marc griped, irritated that his brother had brought some mangy dog to his wedding. "Go get the dog, Bruce."

Marc disappeared into the garage and returned with a thin rope he'd used to stake up some plants. Bruce came around the house holding a filthy medium-sized dog with matted fur.

"Oh my God. That dog stinks," Marc said, waving his hand in front of his face. "He needs a bath. And he's ruining your suit."

"Can I use your hose?" Bruce asked.

"Won't you get your suit wet?" Ravyn asked.

"Come with me to the house," Marc said, angrily. "Take your suit off and put on a pair of my shorts and a T-shirt."

"I'll iron your suit, Bruce," Ravyn said, trying to be helpful.

Julie had walked up and put her hand on Ravyn's arm. "I'll iron his suit. You have a rehearsal to attend."

"But you need to be in the rehearsal, too," Ravyn said.

"I guarantee you I can iron that suit quicker than you. I have my husband's shirts to iron every week and I can press those pants and jacket. But do you have some Febreze? I'm not sure if I'm going to spray the dog or the suit."

"Spray both," Marc growled.

Marc, Julie and Bruce disappeared into the house after the dog was tied to a nearby tree. When Bruce came out of the house in a T-shirt and shorts, he used dish soap, water and a cloth to clean the stray as best he could. The dog shook himself dry, getting Bruce wet.

Bruce then tied the dog up to the tent pole, moving the fan to blow next to him. He returned to the house and re-emerged into the backyard in a pressed suit. Julie came out behind him with a thumbs up signal and a big grin on her face.

"Told you I could be quick about it," she said.

Marc rounded up the wedding party for the quick rehearsal walk through. Julie and Bruce came down the aisle, followed by Jane and Clay O'Connor. Julie's daughters Lexie and Ashley came down the aisle together pretending to drop the rose petals from their white wicker baskets.

Then Ravyn and her father John came down the aisle. The minister quickly glossed over the vows and said he'd see them in about an hour for the real ceremony.

Marc looked at Ravyn, who had turned pale. "You OK?"

Ravyn shook her head and bolted for the house.

"Oh no," Julie said, following Ravyn into the house. She could hear Ravyn being sick in the bathroom.

"Sweetie, I'll get you some crackers."

"And Sprite," Ravyn coughed.

Ravyn emerged from the bathroom with a cold washcloth on her neck. She'd wanted to wipe her face but knew that would ruin her makeup.

Julie opened the can of Sprite and handed it over. "What can I do for you?"

"I need to get my wedding dress on. Help me get this dress off without messing up my hair."

"You've got it. Here, sit on the edge of the bed. I don't want you fainting on me."

Julie unzipped the dress, then lifted the dress up to Ravyn's waist as Ravyn sat down. "Now bend over a bit and put your arms out."

Julie gently lifted the sundress off and took the wedding dress out of its garment bag. "I'd forgotten how beautiful this dress is. You're going to knock Marc out."

Julie helped Ravyn get the new dress on, then touched up her makeup and hair.

"You are beautiful, Ravyn," she said, hugging her friend.

"Love you."

"Love you, too. Now let's get you married."

The guests were seated when Julie and Bruce began their walk down the aisle again, followed by Jane and Clay. Lexie and Ashley again came down the aisle, this time, dropping red rose petals on the white satin fabric draped between the guest chairs. John opened the back door with Ravyn on his arm.

Marc sucked in a sharp intake of breath when he saw Ravyn in her wedding dress. He'd never seen her so beautiful. He made a little noise in the back of his throat and Clay looked over at him.

"You OK, bro?" Clay asked.

Marc could only nod. He was trying hard to keep his emotions in check.

When Ravyn finally stood at his side, Marc felt his mouth go dry and his eyes begin to water. He took her hand and looked in her eyes as the minister asked Ravyn to recite the vows.

"I, Ravyn, take you, Marc, to be my husband. I promise to be true to you in good times and in bad, in sickness and in health. I will love and honor you all the days of my life."

"I, Marc," he began, then cleared his throat. "I, Marc, take you, Ravyn, to be my wife." He choked on the word "wife" but gathered himself and continued. "I promise to be true to you in good times and in bad, in sickness and in health. I will love and honor you all the days of my life."

Ravyn had tears streaming down her face. She bit her bottom lip, trying to stop her tears so she wouldn't ruin her makeup.

"You have the rings to exchange?" the minister asked and Clay produced the rings from his pocket.

Marc placed the ring on Ravyn's finger. "With this ring, I wed you and pledge you my love now and forever."

Ravyn's hands shook as she held Marc's hand as she repeated the ring vows and placed his ring on his left hand.

"You have pledged your love among your family and witnesses," the minister said. "By the power vested in me, and the County of Fulton, I now pronounce you husband and wife."

Marc pulled Ravyn into him, kissing her for a long time.

"Hey, buddy!" Clay cracked. "Save something for the wedding night!"

The wedding guests clapped and hooted. Ravyn could feel her face turn red. Marc was grinning broadly.

Clay came up and clapped him on the back and Jane and Julie rushed to hug Ravyn.

Bruce's stray dog began barking at the excited guests, straining on the thin rope. Suddenly, the dog's weight bent the tent pole, making one corner of the tent sag deeply.

"Oh shit!" Marc yelled, pulling Ravyn to him to protect her.

Startled, Julie and Jane both screamed. Jane stepped back and knocked over the tall vase holding the calla lilies. The vase tipped from its pedestal and water poured into the fan closest to the dog. The fan shorted out and caught fire, shooting flames up the corner of the canvas tent.

All hell broke loose then. The dog, frightened by the fire, broke the rope and then the tent pole. The dog began barking wildly at the flaming fan, running between and around the guests and their legs.

"Call 911!" someone shouted. "Call 911!"

"Oh my God! The tent is on fire!" a woman screamed.

"I've got 911 on the phone. What's the address?" another guest called out.

Bruce ran over to the garden hose he'd used earlier that afternoon to clean the dog and began spraying the fan, putting out the fire on the fan and then the corner of the tent that was also aflame. For good measure Bruce stamped out the burnt edges of the tent and unplugged the fan.

Five minutes later, emergency sirens could be heard coming closer and soon firefighters jumped from the fire engine with hoses in their hands.

"Oh! You guys again," one firefighter said. "We thought this address was familiar."

"I think we've got it under control, sir," Bruce said, still spraying water on the tent and fan.

"Thanks for putting out the fire, Bruce," Marc said, putting his arm around his brother. "Good thinking going for the garden hose."

The firefighters sprayed some foam on the fan and the tent. The air smelled of burnt plastic and canvas. The firefighters congratulated Marc and Ravyn on their wedding, then rolled up their hoses and left the house.

"I don't think we're getting our deposit back on the tent," Ravyn said, looking at the foamy mess and laughing.

"You know, there wasn't a fire at my wedding!" Jane teased.

"Oh my! This was quite the excitement," Kaye said, fanning herself with a small paper fan the caterers had placed on all of the chairs. The logo of the catering service was printed on both sides. "Are you OK?" she asked her daughter. Ravyn nodded.

The excitement quelled, guests began gathering around the food on the caterer's tables. Chafing dish covers were lifted and guests loaded food onto white plastic plates.

Ravyn heard a cork pop and caterers began to hand out flutes of champagne.

Bruce tossed a small roll to the scruffy dog, who grabbed it without letting it hit the ground. "I think I'm going to name him Blaze."

"Hey, no feeding the expensive food to that mutt!" Marc yelled, but he was smiling.

"Blaze," Bruce corrected, looking down to see the dog scratching his ear with his hind leg. Then Blaze began licking himself.

"You can feed Blaze. There's more roast beef. There's even some prime rib," Ravyn told Bruce, punching Marc playfully on the arm. "Your brother saved the wedding."

"No giving that dog prime rib! And he didn't save the wedding; he just put out the fire, which that mangy dog caused."

"And your brother saved the wedding."

Marc rolled his eyes. "OK, OK, he saved the wedding." He handed Ravyn a flute of bubbly liquid, but she could smell it was sparkling cider. She put her hand on her abdomen and smiled up at him. He moved his hand over hers entwining her fingers with his.

"A toast to the new couple!"

"Cheers!"

Marc pulled Ravyn in close again. "To us," he said, clinking his glass to hers. "I don't know if I could love you any more than I do right now. My life was empty until I met you. You were my missing puzzle piece, Ravyn. I know when I wake up tomorrow morning, I'll love you even more than I do today. Every day after that I'll love you just a little bit more. To us, Ravyn, to our new family."

Made in the USA
Monee, IL
26 May 2021

68719485R00125